I0745102

Carter

TWILIGHT FALLS BOOK TWO

A.M. SALINGER

COPYRIGHT

Carter (Twilight Falls #2)
Copyright © 2019 by A.M. Salinger
All rights reserved. Registered with the US Copyright Office.
Second paperback edition: 2024
ISBN: 978-1-9162270-0-2

www.AMSalinger.com
shop.adstarrling.com

Edited by www.ElfwerksEditing.com
Cover Design by A.M. Salinger

BOOKS BY A.M. SALINGER

NIGHTS

One Night - 1

The Escort - 2

Tokyo Heat - 3

Sweet Obsession - 4

Sweet Possession - 5

The Proposition - 6

Undisclosed - 7

Hush - 8

One Day - 9

TWILIGHT FALLS

Alex - 1

Carter - 2

Hunter - 3

Wyatt - 4

Drake - 5

Tristan - 6

Miles - 7

CHAPTER ONE

Carter Wilson closed his eyes and groaned as he came in the mouth of the woman who was busy blowing him. His fingers clenched in her perfectly-styled hair, messing it up. He knew it would likely give away what they'd been up to, but he didn't care.

A hiss of air left him when she finally let go of his pleasantly spent cock. The blonde sat back on her expensive Jimmy Choo heels and licked her lips greedily as she gazed up at him, her blue eyes sultry with lust and her nipples hard where her breasts showed in her gaping cleavage.

Carter reluctantly tucked his dick back in his tuxedo trousers.

If he'd had a condom on him, he would have pulled her to her feet, yanked up her thousand-dollar Dolce & Gabbana dress, and fucked her against the wall of the art gallery's restroom stall until she screamed in pleasure.

He'd unfortunately used the last rubber in his wallet

in his trailer yesterday, after he finished shooting what he hoped would be his next Hollywood blockbuster movie in New York. He'd known that the assistant he'd been given by the studio had had the hots for him all along, but Carter never liked mixing business with pleasure, not after the unpleasant incident that had nearly ended his movie career prematurely. So he'd waited until the last day of filming to give her a parting gift, which was his dick in her mouth and her hungry pussy.

Most people called him a bastard and a serial womanizer, a reputation that was only rendered more infamous by the paparazzi who constantly tailed him. Carter didn't mind. He knew the career he'd chosen meant sacrificing his privacy and, as far as he was concerned, his conscience was clear; he'd never made false promises to the women he'd slept with, always used protection, and had been upfront about never wanting to be in a serious relationship.

There were only two aspects of his life that Carter protected jealously: his family and his hidden bisexuality. The first had been surprisingly easy to keep under wraps, since his only living relative had left the small town they'd grown up in some years back and was now halfway across the world.

As for the second, although there were plenty of gay actors who'd come out in the business in the last few decades, Carter knew his status as an action hero and the opportunities that might come his way in the future might be affected if he were to reveal like he liked to fuck men as much as he liked fucking women.

On the occasions when he felt like dick more than pussy, Carter visited an exclusive club in L.A. where all employees and guests were made to sign non-disclosure agreements. There, he had his pick of the male clientele who habitually called upon the club to satisfy their own secret desires. Carter had been hesitant to join up at first. But after hearing the club rules dictated all visitors wear close-fitting carnival masks to conceal their identities and that there were private suites where guests could indulge in their wildest sexual fantasies, he'd signed on the dotted line and never regretted it since.

"I think it's about time we got back out there, don't you?" Carter told the blonde with a relaxed grin.

She hesitated before returning his smile with a lingering look of regret. Carter knew she would brag to her closest friends about tonight. It wasn't everyday she got to suck the cock of a A-list Hollywood star while her husband was entertaining their guests fifty feet away.

Carter waited a couple of minutes after she vacated the restroom before stepping out into the service corridor at the rear of the art gallery. He stilled when he saw the woman leaning a hip against the wall in the shadows, her arms crossed rigidly across her body.

Izzy Batista's green eyes were dark with exasperation and there was a distinctly unhappy moue on her pretty face. "Please tell me you didn't just fuck the gallery owner's wife?"

Carter's lips tilted in a teasing smirk. "It depends on your definition of fuck."

Izzy swore. "For Christ's sake Carter, can't you keep it in your pants for one goddamn night?!"

Carter strolled up to her and rested his shoulder casually against the wall, mimicking her pose.

"Normally, I would say yes," he drawled in a sarcastic tone. "But, you see, a little mouse with brown hair and green eyes blackmailed me into coming here and I just had to, you know, *blow* off some steam."

Izzy rolled her eyes. "It's only for a couple of hours. Besides, your agent said you didn't have anything lined up for tonight."

Carter frowned. "I did have something lined up. It was called an evening spent relaxing in my own home for the first time in three months."

Izzy gasped and raised a hand to her lips, an expression of mock horror painted across her face. "OMG! Is this the first sign that Carter Wilson is getting old? Would you like me to get you slippers and a hot cocoa kit for Christmas?"

"Ha-ha, very funny," Carter muttered.

Izzy grinned and tucked her arm through his elbow. "Now, why don't you be a good blackmail victim and come along peacefully. We're about to do the big reveal."

Carter grunted and allowed her to guide him to the main gallery area.

Izzy was the younger sister of Wyatt Batista, one of Carter's closest childhood friends from his hometown of Twilight Falls. Together with Tristan Hart, Hunter Thomson, Drake Jackson, Miles Martinez, and Alex Hancock, they'd formed the "Terrible Seven", a name that had struck dread in the heart of parents, teachers, and law enforcement for the decade and a half they'd grown up together in the quaint tourist town in the San Bernardino Mountains.

It was Izzy who'd sneaked in the boy's locker room when Carter and the others were in high school and taken the infamous picture of his naked butt, which she had threatened to use to blackmail him on many an occasion since.

Though Carter knew it was in jest, he still worried about Izzy. The woman was the devil incarnate when it came to poking fun at her friends, and Carter wouldn't put it past her to one day find a picture of his sixteen-year-old ass plastered over a billboard in L.A.

A dull murmur of voices reached them as they turned a corner and entered the gallery. Tonight was the opening night of Finn West's first art exhibition in over three years and the whole town was buzzing with the return of the famous artist.

Although Carter had reluctantly agreed to headline the guest list, he had to admit to being more than a little intrigued once Izzy explained the circumstances behind her request.

It turned out Finn was Alex Hancock's husband of a few months.

Carter's gaze found the happy couple where they stood with the art gallery owner next the central piece of the exhibition, which still lay hidden beneath a white sheet. Finn had seemed tense when Carter had met him on the red carpet at the beginning of the evening. He now looked like a totally different person and could hardly keep his eyes, and his hands, off the man next to him.

A twinge of jealousy stabbed through Carter as he observed Alex's radiant expression. It was evident to anyone in the room that the pair were very much in love. He wondered if he would ever find that kind of connection one day, or if he was doomed to a life of brief sexual encounters.

Carter had yet to meet anyone who had held his sexual and intellectual interest long enough for him to consider them as a potential life partner. The women who entered his life seemed more interested in having a movie star as a boyfriend than in who he was as a person, while the men were one-night stands whose faces he wouldn't recognize if he passed them on the street.

He smiled blankly at the art gallery's owner's wife as he walked past the couple and let Izzy lead him to Finn and Alex's side. Alex greeted him with a hug and a hearty pat on the back and Carter found himself feeling genuinely happy for his friend as he embraced him. They'd all been through some rough times together before he and Alex left Twilight Falls and it was great to see Alex's eyes devoid of the guilt he'd carried for so many years.

The central piece of the exhibition was finally revealed to wild applause. Carter took his leave an hour later and headed out of the back door to the parking lot. He'd just climbed inside his Maserati when his cell started ringing. He took the phone out of his pocket and stared at the screen.

It was an international number. One he didn't recognize.

The first tendril of dread pooled inside Carter as he gazed at it. He hesitated before taking the call. "Hello?"

"Is that Mr. Wilson? Mr. Carter Wilson?" a woman said in a heavy French accent. "The next of kin of Louise Payton?"

Carter's stomach clenched in fear. "Yes, it is," he finally managed, mouth so dry he was surprised he didn't croak.

"I'm so sorry, Mr. Wilson," the woman continued in a voice filled with compassion, "I'm afraid there has been a terrible accident."

A buzzing noise filled Carter's ears. The words the woman was saying reached him dimly, every syllable a knife that stabbed into his heart.

In that moment, he knew his life would never be the same again.

CHAPTER TWO

Elijah Davis finished polishing the shiny, new stainless-steel work tables in the center of the kitchen and took off his apron. He turned in a slow circle and studied the industrial-sized ovens, the commercial proofer, the chiller, the walk-in freezer, the shelves holding trays, tins, pans, and racks, and the professional mixers sitting on a counter with a critical eye.

A slow grin split his face. He'd finally done it.

The swing door opened. A young woman with short, pink and blue hair and half a dozen piercings strolled in, a tired smile on her face.

"I think we're ready," Sam Harris said with a confident dip of her chin.

She joined Elijah and stared around the lovingly restored kitchen. The butcher's block they'd bought for a bargain at a garage sale a month ago had come up beautifully after some sanding and took pride of place between the metal tables in the middle of the room.

They'd spent one weekend stripping decades of greased-up paint from the cabinets and cupboards before whitewashing them and applying thick coats of cream and duck egg blue. The colors matched the bakery's new facade and the shop's gaily decorated interior.

La Petite Bouche Gourmande was officially opening for business tomorrow.

"Bet you're excited," Sam told Elijah with a grin, exposing a slightly crooked tooth.

"So much so I don't think I'm gonna sleep tonight," Elijah admitted fervently.

"Well, I'd offer to help you with that, but you like dicks and I like pussies, so our work affair is unfortunately doomed before it can even begin."

Elijah chuckled at her deadpan expression.

It still surprised him how completely wrong his first impression of Sam had been. When he'd first laid eyes on her on the day she came to interview for the position of his bakery manager, he'd already resigned himself to hiring somebody out of town for the job.

Although Twilight Falls wasn't exactly famous for producing pâtissiers, he'd hoped to at least find someone competent enough to handle a basic kitchen and a cake shop.

Elijah's heart had sunk when Sam had walked into the office above the bakery and sat down on the other side of the desk, a faintly mutinous expression on her flushed face. He'd told himself he would indulge her since she was the last interviewee of the day and had nearly fallen out of his chair after she correctly told him the steps required to make macarons five minutes later.

It was afterward that Sam told him she was so used to people assuming she was unreliable because of her appearance that she normally went in with all guns blazing.

Elijah had given her the job on the spot.

"It still feels strange, you know," Sam mused. "When I first saw your ad, I didn't believe my eyes for a second. Why would a renowned pastry chef leave a Michelin-star restaurant and a successful career in Paris to open a bakery in the back end of nowhere?" A teasing light warmed her face. "And not just any pastry chef, but a hot one, with a body like Adonis."

Elijah pressed a hand to his heart with an expression of fake shock. "You think I'm hot? And that I look like Adonis?"

Sam rolled her eyes. "I take it back. Your ego doesn't need any more inflating."

They closed up shop a short while later.

"Be careful," Elijah told Sam as she climbed on her moped.

She saluted and headed off in the night. Elijah watched her until she disappeared and turned to gaze at the bakery's facade. A melancholic feeling swirled through him as he studied the freshly painted shop sign.

La Petite Bouche Gourmande had been one of his favorite children's books. His most vivid memories of his maternal, French grandmother were of her reading it to him during the long summers his family spent in France when he was growing up.

"Because I made a promise to someone very important to me," Elijah said quietly, finally answering the question Sam had asked him.

Elijah's grandmother had come to Twilight Falls only once, when he was fifteen. She had immediately fallen in love with the picturesque town, which was as different from the sleepy French village she had spent most of her life in as night was from day. It was during that trip that they'd spoken of his future and Elijah had first told her his dreams of going to Paris to study to be a professional pâtissier, a dream he had so far hidden from his own parents. His grandmother had been quiet for some time as they strolled through the town. Then, she'd stopped and pointed out a charming coffee shop.

"Like that," she'd said in her heavily accented English. "You should come back and open a bakery here just like that, in this beautiful place." She'd gazed at the forested valley draped in autumnal colors that surrounded Twilight Falls, before beaming at him. "You will be happy here. I can feel it."

She had planned to visit again but had fallen ill shortly after his seventeenth birthday and passed away on the night Elijah and his mother arrived in France to see her. They'd spent a couple of weeks after her funeral organizing her affairs before returning to Twilight Falls with a box full of her personal items. Among them had been the book she had read to Elijah when he was still a boy and the one thing of hers he'd taken with him when he'd left for Paris a few years later.

It was close to eleven by the time Elijah got home. His parents were away on their long-awaited world cruise and had given him the keys to their house while he settled back into town and looked for his own place. He parked his vintage, pea-green Citroën DS on the driveway at the end of the cul-de-sac where they'd moved to and was climbing the steps to the front porch when a child's faint cry reached him.

Elijah turned and was surprised to see lights in the pretty, white clapboard house across the way. His father had given him the impression the place was empty. Not that it bothered Elijah to have neighbors. The properties on the estate had generous plots and were mostly occupied by retired folks.

A shadow moved across a window on the second floor.

From the distance, Elijah made out the figure of a man rocking a little girl with blonde hair in his arms. The man stopped and turned to look straight at him.

Elijah flushed at being caught staring. He realized belatedly that the guy probably couldn't see him where he stood in the dark. He twisted on his heels and headed inside his parents' house, curious as to who it was who'd moved in opposite him.

CHAPTER THREE

"Thanks," Elijah muttered. He finished folding the last puff pastry dough, wrapped the batch in cling film, and popped them in the chiller.

Sam handed him a cup of freshly brewed coffee. Elijah inhaled the smoky scent of roasted French beans and savored the first sip with a tired sigh.

"You make the best coffee."

"You buy the best coffee beans." Sam frowned. "So, what's up? The opening was a success and we sold out within two hours. I know it's only been three days, but I thought you'd still be on cloud nine. By the way, I think we're gonna need another pair of hands out front if things stay as they are. Daisy is working herself ragged serving the tables and I'm too busy behind the counter to help her."

Elijah rubbed the back of his neck and winced at his stiff muscles. "I'm not getting much sleep. And I agree.

I thought we might have to hire a second waitress down the line. I didn't expect it would be this soon."

"What can I say? You make the best cakes on the West Coast and, according to most of the women who visited the shop today, you're sex on legs." Sam raised an eyebrow. "Why the lack of sleep? Too much fornicating?"

Elijah groaned. "I wish. Besides, I've been single since I moved here."

"There are toys, Elijah," Sam said bluntly.

"I worry about you." Elijah paused and pursed his lips. "My new neighbors have a child who cries a lot at night."

"Oh." Sam raised an eyebrow. "Have you spoken to them about it?"

"Not yet," Elijah murmured. "It looks like they're struggling. Although, I've not really seen the mom."

"You tried earplugs?" Sam said.

"I might have to resort to that soon," Elijah admitted.

They closed shop a few hours later and headed their separate ways. Elijah considered dining out before belatedly remembering the steak he had marinating in his parents' refrigerator.

God, I must really be tired.

He drove home, pulled up outside his parents' house, and glanced at the lights blazing out of the property opposite the road. There was a car parked at an angle on the drive, as if its owner had come home in a hurry. It was a flashy, yellow Maserati.

Elijah frowned.

Not exactly child friendly.

He went inside, had the steak with a large glass of Cabernet Sauvignon, and plopped down on the couch in the living room to catch a late night replay of a baseball game. He must have fallen asleep as the next thing he knew, a loud shriek jolted him awake. He bolted upright and almost fell off the couch.

"What the—"

One of the windows facing out front was open. A faint breeze stirred the curtains. It brought with it the sound of crying.

Elijah stared through the glass at the house across the way.

The scream came again.

He jumped up, snatched his cell and house keys, and ran outside. He was across the road in seconds, took the porch stairs two steps at a time, and started pressing the doorbell and banging on the door.

"Hey! Is everything okay?!"

A child's sobs rose above the sound of the chimes of the bell from somewhere inside the property.

Lights were coming on in the adjacent house. An elderly couple appeared at a window, faces pale, the woman's hands clutching the top of her nightgown at her throat.

Elijah gave them a reassuring wave where he stood under the porch light and resumed knocking on the door.

The child's crying suddenly stopped.

A chill filled his veins. Elijah wavered between calling the cops and kicking the damn door open. He'd just raised his fist to strike it for the final time when it opened unexpectedly.

Elijah stumbled and almost fell inside. He grabbed the frame and righted himself at the last second before staring at the man in the doorway.

The guy was six feet tall, had dirty blond hair, arresting hazel eyes that were currently glazed over with a mixture of exhaustion and frustration, and a body and a face to die for.

Elijah's gaze dropped to the red blotches smeared across the man's white T-shirt and the bread knife in his hand. His stomach clenched with fear.

Shit! Is that—blood?!

A low sob and a sniffle came from somewhere behind the guy. Anger overcame Elijah's dread. He drew his arm back and punched the guy in the face.

"You bastard!" Elijah stormed inside the house, aware he was doing something stupidly crazy. "Where is she?!"

A hiccup came from down a hallway decorated in pale pastels. Elijah followed the sound to the back of the house, his knuckles throbbing. The man mumbled something incoherent and followed in his footsteps.

Elijah entered a modern kitchen-diner that overlooked the property's rear garden and the evergreen forest that backed onto it, glanced around, and staggered to a stop, his eyes rounding.

The little girl with the blonde hair stood in the middle of the room, a teddy bear with tattered ears and limbs in one hand and an upended bottle of ketchup in the other. There was a petulant expression on her face.

Elijah's gaze moved from the puddles of red sauce on the floor, to the remains of what looked like a butchered hot dog on a plate on the black marble island.

"What on earth is going on?"

Fresh tears gathered in the little girl's blue eyes. She let out a loud bawl.

CHAPTER FOUR

CARTER'S STOMACH TWISTED AS MAISIE'S CRIES ECHOED around the kitchen once more. He put the bread knife on the counter, crossed the floor, and went down on his knees, heedless of the ketchup making a mess of his jeans and the pain pulsing through his jaw. He gathered the little girl in his arms and felt his heart break at the way she trembled in his hold.

"There, there, it's all right, sweetheart," he hushed softly.

Carter spared a glance for the man who'd just hit him and barged inside his home uninvited. He didn't know who the guy was and, right now, he didn't care. He was, quite frankly, at his wits' end.

It had been ten days since he'd moved from L.A. to his dead sister's house in Twilight Falls. Louise and Mark had bought the place and fixed it up when they first got married. It had become more of a holiday home since, what with the couple having lived in Washington for several years before their more recent relocation to Brussels for Mark's new job at the U.S. Consulate.

Six weeks had passed since the terrible night Carter had learned of the couple's death in a car accident in the Belgian capital. After calling his agent to cancel all his immediate engagements, Carter had packed a bag and flown out to Europe.

Maisie, Carter's niece and the little girl he had only ever seen in photographs and on video chats, had been with a neighbor at the time of the accident.

It was Carter who had had to fetch her from the woman's house and tell her, in a voice that broke with his own grief, that her mommy and daddy were not coming home. It had taken several days for the truth to sink in. By then, Carter had already buried Louise and Mark.

To his shock, the couple's will officially named him as Maisie's guardian if anything were to happen to them. Still, Carter had made the effort to reach out to Mark's immediate family. It turned out Mark's estranged brother wanted nothing to do with the little girl, and his parents, who lived in Texas, were too riddled with health problems to care for her either.

Mark's colleagues at the consulate had been more than eager to speed up the paperwork for Maisie's guardianship and assist Carter in making the necessary arrangements for the little girl to return to California with him.

And thus begun four weeks of hell. It started with nightmares and rapidly progressed to screaming tantrums that kept Carter awake all hours of the night.

Luckily, he was between projects and wasn't scheduled to start work on his next movie until the end of the following month. After days of trying to comfort the little girl and even hiring a nanny to assist him in caring for her, Carter had finally taken Maisie to see a children's therapist.

To Carter's dismay, Maisie was diagnosed with a form of post traumatic stress disorder and severe separation anxiety. Though she was able to show genuine affection for Carter, the loss of her parents had been too abrupt for her to fully accept him as her caregiver and she was still grieving. The fact that she had reverted to speaking mainly French and rarely uttered anything in English only served to prove the therapist's point.

Under the woman's recommendations, Carter devoted himself to making as a stable a life as he possibly could to provide Maisie with a sense of security. Although he'd stuck to the therapist's suggested routines for meals and bedtime, the one thing he'd struggled with from the get go though was setting limits for the little girl. All it took was one look at Maisie's beautiful, tear-filled eyes, which reminded him so much of his own sister's expressive ones, and Carter often found himself caving in to the little girl's demands, however impractical they were.

It was Maisie's therapist who had suggested to Carter that relocating to somewhere the little girl might feel safer could prove to be key to her wellbeing. His life as a movie star meant he could hardly take Maisie out without being followed and hounded by the paparazzi everywhere they went, and Carter had found himself close to beating up more than one prying asshole when they'd scared his niece with their flashing cameras.

The phone call from Izzy had almost come as a sign.

"Jesus, Carter! Seriously?! I only found out about Louise and Mark today, when I was speaking to a reporter friend!" *Izzy said, aghast. "Why didn't you tell us?!"*

Carter had just put Maisie to bed. He closed the door to the little girl's bedroom, headed down the stairs of his modern, beachfront, Malibu home and walked out onto the terrace.

"A lot has happened, Izzy." He rested his elbows on the railing and rubbed a hand down his face, too tired to even grimace at the stubble peppering his cheeks and jawline. "To be honest, it still hasn't sunk in." He swallowed past the sudden lump in his throat. "That she's gone."

Izzy had stayed quiet for a moment. "I'm so sorry, Carter," she finally murmured, her voice trembling. "I know how close you were to Louise. She was my friend too."

Carter's vision blurred as he looked out over the dark ocean. Izzy had been a high school freshman when Louise was a sophomore. Later that same year, Carter and Louise's mother was diagnosed with severe MS. She didn't live to see Louise graduate from college. It wasn't long after that their father followed their mother to the grave. Though the coroner stated he'd died of a massive coronary, Carter and Louise had known it was from a broken heart. Their parents had been childhood sweethearts and had never spent a single day apart in over fifty years.

"Is there anything I can do to help? That we can do?" Izzy said.

Carter knew she meant the guys he'd grown up with. As the faces of his close friends swam before his eyes, he found himself overwhelmed with emotion and spilling his guts out to Izzy. He told her everything. About Maisie's nightmares and outbursts. About what the therapist had said. About the fact that he was proving to be a failure as Maisie's guardian and uncle.

"You're not a failure," Izzy murmured. "God, Carter, I can't even begin to imagine the hell you've been going through. You haven't had time to grieve yourself."

Carter remained silent at that. He was aware he still needed to work through his own feelings about Louise and Mark's deaths.

"Come home, Carter," Izzy said quietly.

Carter stared at the phosphorescent surf crashing onto the shoreline. "What?"

"I said, come home. To Twilight Falls. The pace of life is slower here, and you and Maisie can get to know each other better. Besides, didn't Louise and Mark have a house here?"

Carter raked a hand through his hair. It was a crazy idea. And the more he thought about it, the better it started to sound.

"You'll breathe easier here, Carter. Everyone's known you since you were a shitty, little snot-nosed brat and will respect your privacy. Besides, the guys and I can help. And L.A. isn't far away."

Carter grimaced. "I wasn't that shitty. Or little."

"You were the worst of the bunch and you know it," Izzy stated adamantly. "It was that cutesy smile of yours that got

you out of trouble all the time. And I hardly think we should be addressing the size of your dick right now."

Carter's lips twitched as he relaxed in the casual banter. "It's pretty big. And you think my smile is cute?"

"If Wyatt knew you were flirting with me, he'd beat your ass up," Izzy said tartly.

It had taken Carter a good few days to convince his agent that the move was necessary. And so, just over a month after he brought Maisie to L.A., he closed up house and headed off to the San Bernardino Mountains and Twilight Falls.

Although Izzy and the guys had been true to their word, even Alex and Finn visiting and helping out despite the fact that they were just settling into their new relationship, Maisie had been wary of strangers in their new home and had become even more clingy, to the point she'd point blank refused to leave the house these past three days.

Carter had suspected Izzy and Wyatt would have a heck of a time with her when he'd gone to L.A. that afternoon to sign a contract with a studio. He'd come home at eight to the sound of Maisie's weeping, the heartrending sobs carrying clearly through the open windows of the house, and had parked hastily on the drive before rushing inside, only to find her crying in Izzy's arms while Wyatt looked on helplessly.

The way Maisie had practically launched herself at Carter the moment he'd walked through the door had made him feel like a cad. He'd cursed himself for making the trip when he knew the little girl's separation anxiety was still an issue.

"Are you going to be okay?" Wyatt had murmured as he and Izzy got ready to leave.

Carter had nodded tiredly. "Yeah. I'm going to give her a bath and put her to bed."

All his friends knew about Maisie seeing a therapist and it was clear to Carter that they were just as worried about his niece as he was.

Maisie had gone down surprisingly easily, no doubt exhausted by the stress of that day. For a moment, Carter had thought she might even sleep through the night. That hope was dashed when she woke up from a nightmare two hours later. Tired and hungry, she'd insisted on Carter making them hot dogs. Luckily, he'd had some in the freezer.

The trouble started when he refused to hand her the bread knife so she could help.

CHAPTER FIVE

Surprise filled Elijah as he stood watching the man and his daughter. He was beginning to realize that what he'd heard earlier was the little girl having an almighty hissy fit; it was clear from the way she was clinging to her father and he to her that they cared deeply for one another. His heart sank.

Damn. I really owe him an apology for hitting him.

Elijah was about to voice just that when the little girl hiccupped, snot and tears streaming down her face.

"Je veux des hot dogs!" she wailed into her father's chest.

Elijah startled. *They're French?* He frowned. *That can't be right. Her father has a distinctly local accent.*

"Where's her mom?"

The man stiffened at Elijah's question. The little girl raised her head and stared at Elijah over his shoulder.

"Maman et papa sont au paradis," she said in a small, matter-of-fact voice. She wiped her eyes. *"Qui es-tu?"*

A sick feeling twisted Elijah's stomach as the man

rose to his feet and turned, his hand resting protectively on the little girl's head where she stood clinging to his leg. His beautiful eyes were dull and lifeless.

"Her parents are dead," he explained in the awkward hush, answering Elijah's mute question and confirming what the little girl had said. "I'm her uncle."

Suddenly, it all made sense. Elijah cursed himself once more for having thought the worse of his neighbor over the past few days. "It's just the two of you?"

The man hesitated before nodding.

A sniffle drew their gazes to the little girl. Fresh tears were welling up in her eyes and she looked close to bawling again.

"*Tu veux des hot dogs, ma puce?*" Elijah said gently.

The little girl's mouth went slack, as did her uncle's.

Elijah bit his lip to stop the bark of laughter suddenly bubbling up his throat at their identical shocked looks.

"Do you have more bread and hot dogs?" he asked the guy, straight faced.

"Sure." The man indicated the refrigerator. "I'm Carter, by the way. This is Maisie."

Elijah smiled at the pair. ""Nice to meet you. I'm Elijah, your neighbor across the road." He flashed an apologetic grimace at Carter. "And sorry about hitting you. We should get some ice on that."

"No problem." Carter wriggled his jaw from side to side. A wry smile curved his lips. "You pack quite a punch."

Elijah's pulse jumped. Carter's smile transformed his face from gorgeous to downright breathtaking.

Maisie shifted slightly from her uncle's side and stared unblinkingly at Elijah. Her gaze dropped.

"You have no shoes?" she asked hesitantly.

Elijah realized his feet were bare. "Oh. I forgot to grab them when I rushed out of the house."

He looked up and almost startled at the expression on Carter's face. The man was staring at the little girl as if he'd seen a ghost.

"You spoke in English," Carter mumbled.

Maisie wiped her nose on the back of her hand and nodded vigorously, looking strangely proud of herself. From the emotion clouding Carter's eyes, Elijah suspected there was a story behind that statement.

"Why don't you two clean up while I get the hot dogs ready?"

Carter blinked at him before glancing at the ketchup streaked across his T-shirt and jeans. "Sure."

Twenty minutes later, Carter and Maisie sat at the now spotless kitchen island and gazed in awe at the perfect French hot dogs and fries laid out on plates before them, Carter holding a pack of ice wrapped in a towel to his face.

Elijah suppressed a grin at their expressions.

They're like peas in a pod.

"Dig in."

They did just that, Maisie following her uncle's lead and picking daintily at her food so as not to spill any mustard.

"Are you a god?" Carter groaned around a mouthful

of bread and sausage. "Because these are the best hot dogs I've ever tasted."

Maisie nodded mutely, her cheeks bulging and her eyes bright with delight.

A warm feeling filled Elijah's chest. Seeing other people enjoy the food he made was one of the reasons he'd become a chef. He bit into his own hot dog and sighed as the tangy mustard and fried onions hit his taste buds. Even though he was still full from his steak dinner, both Carter and Maisie had insisted he make one for himself.

Elijah swallowed and smiled. "I'm glad you like it."

Carter paused and stared at Elijah.

"Is everything okay?" Elijah said, puzzled.

"Yeah." Carter carried on eating, the strange expression fading from his face.

Maisie started yawning soon after finishing her late night snack.

"Time to go back to bed, sweetheart." Carter finished washing up, dried his hands, and came around the island.

Maisie looped her arms around his neck when he lifted her from the bar stool.

"I don't want to. *Je vais faire des cauchemars,*" she protested feebly. She stuck her thumb in her mouth, her sleepy face overshadowed by apprehension.

Carter's eyes darkened with dismay.

Elijah understood once again why it was the little girl cried so much at night. "Do you want me to read you a bedtime story?"

Carter and Maisie stared at him. Elijah cursed

himself, regretting his impulsive offer. He'd intruded enough on their time as it was and it was close to midnight.

"I'm sorry," he mumbled, "that was—"

"Do you know one in French?" Carter interrupted, his tone hopeful.

"*Oui?*" Maisie murmured questioningly, her blue eyes brightening slightly.

Elijah hesitated before nodding, strangely relieved they hadn't refused him. He followed them upstairs and sat on the edge of Maisie's bed while Carter helped her brush her teeth and tucked her in.

Maisie hugged her ragged teddy bear to her chest and listened drowsily while Elijah quietly told her the story of *La Petite Bouche Gourmande* from memory, using the same singsong voice his grandmother had used to narrate the book when he was a child. She was asleep before he'd finished the tale, her small chest rising and falling slightly with her breaths.

Emotion clogged Elijah's throat as he gazed at her. He rose carefully and followed Carter quietly out of the bedroom.

"Thank you." Carter peered at the sleeping girl with a wistful expression through the gap in the door. "It's so rare for her to settle down this peacefully. I have a battle with her most nights."

Elijah paused on the landing. "How long ago was it? Since she lost them?" He nearly kicked himself when the question hung awkwardly in the silence between them, Carter looking lost and forlorn. "Forgive me, I shouldn't pry. I'll head off home." He started down the stairs, heat flooding his face.

Carter caught up with him in the foyer. "Six weeks."

Elijah stopped and turned. His heart clenched at the sorrow clouding Carter's eyes. "I'm so sorry for your loss."

Carter swallowed and nodded. "I just want Maisie to get better." He rubbed the back of his neck. "I took her to see a therapist when the nightmares and tantrums wouldn't stop. Maisie has a form of PTSD. Her therapist suggested I move from L.A. to settle her somewhere quieter."

Elijah looked past Carter to the hallway. "Is this her parents' house?"

Carter nodded. "Yeah. Louise and Mark bought this place after they met and got married here. Louise was my sister."

Elijah stared. "Wait. You grew up in Twilight Falls?"

Carter's expression turned guarded. "Yes."

"Oh. So did I." Elijah's mouth twisted in an apologetic grimace. "I'm sorry, I can't say I remember you."

Carter blinked, looking stunned for an instant.

"So, how come you speak French?" he said curiously once he recovered.

Ethan wondered at his odd expression once more. "I lived in Paris for a while."

They stepped out onto the porch. Elijah was relieved to see that the house next door was dark, Carter's elderly neighbors having evidently decided not to call the cops and retired for the night.

"And you decided to come back here?" Carter said incredulously. He waved a vague hand at the forest hedging the estate and the surrounding mountains.

Elijah gazed at the stark outlines of the valley bathed in moonlight, a soft smile on his face. "I made a promise to someone. Besides, this place is beautiful, wouldn't you say?"

Carter remained quiet. Elijah turned, puzzled by his silence.

Carter's intense gaze drilled into his face. "Yes, it is."

A wave of self-awareness washed over Elijah. He tried his best not to flush. "I'd better head home." He stepped down the porch stairs, conscious of Carter's hot stare boring into his back.

"I'm sorry you had to come over," Carter called out after him.

Elijah paused and looked over his shoulder. "It's okay."

"And I apologize if I disturbed you and your—" Carter indicated Elijah's home.

Elijah's heart skipped a beat.

If I didn't know any better, I'd think he was fishing.

"That's my parents' house. I just moved back to town."

Carter digested this with an impassive expression. "Oh. Well, thanks again, Elijah."

Even though he did not hear Maisie cry that night, it took a long time for Elijah to fall asleep. And by the time morning came and he dragged himself out of bed and into the bathroom, Elijah was still thinking about

Carter's smile and how his name had sounded on the other man's lips.

CHAPTER SIX

Carter looked up from his cell and stared at Maisie where they sat on the back porch swing. The little girl was coloring, her tongue stuck sweetly out of the corner of her mouth as she concentrated on filling in the cartoon drawing.

It was early evening and they'd just come back from Maisie's counseling session in L.A. Maisie's therapist had recommended a local psychologist take over her treatment to make things easier for Carter in terms of the long commute and she'd just emailed him details of the person she'd proposed.

Carter hesitated, unsure how to take the question. The thing was, he'd also been wondering the same thing. The throbbing on his face made him recall how angry Elijah had looked just before he'd punched him last night.

Angry and hot as fuck.

Much to his embarrassment, Carter felt his cock

stirring, just like it had done when Elijah had smiled at him.

There was no denying that his neighbor was sinfully sexy. With his thick brown hair, chocolate-colored eyes, and honey-tanned skin, Elijah looked like he belonged on a catwalk. Though he was on the lean side, his body was toned and his muscles beautifully defined from what Carter had gleaned when he'd observed him discreetly.

From the way Elijah's ears had reddened just before they parted ways, Carter couldn't help but feel that his neighbor hadn't been completely immune to his charms either.

There was something about Elijah that Carter found, well, riveting.

I wonder if he's gay?

More than curiosity about Elijah's sexual preferences, the thing that still shocked Carter was that Elijah hadn't known who he was. Though he'd only just met the guy, Carter was confident Elijah hadn't lied to him last night when he said he didn't remember him.

Maisie's voice broke through his reverie. "Uncle Carter?" The little girl was frowning. "Do you have a fever? Your face is kinda red."

Carter cursed himself for his lustful musings. "I'm sorry, sweetheart. I'm fine," he mumbled hastily. An idea came to him then. "Should we go ask Elijah over for dinner?"

Maisie brightened. She nodded vigorously. "I want hot dogs again!"

Carter sighed. "We can't have hot dogs every night. Besides, mine aren't anywhere as good as Elijah's."

To his shock, Maisie put down her coloring, scrambled onto her knees, and gave him a hug.

"Your hot dogs are yummy, Uncle Carter." She leaned back and flashed him a winsome smile. "Elijah's are just yummier, is all."

Carter swallowed the lump in his throat. It was rare for Maisie to be so openly affectionate with him. She hadn't had a temper tantrum today either and had woken up refreshed that morning after her first nightmare-free sleep in over a month.

Is it because of Elijah?

"Let's go see if he's back," he murmured.

Carter couldn't help but smile when Maisie took his hand and led the way eagerly through the house. They both startled when she opened the front door.

Elijah was standing on their porch, about to ring the doorbell.

"Hey." He lowered his hand, his face relaxing in a soft expression that made Carter's stomach flutter. "I came to see how you were. And to drop these off."

Carter looked at the box Elijah was holding. It was a pretty shade of cream and duck egg blue, with a logo on top that read *La Petite Bouche Gourmande*.

"I made extra cupcakes today," Elijah explained, his cheeks pinking slightly. "I thought you two might like some for dessert."

Maisie let out a squeal of excitement and jumped up and down, her little hands clapping excitedly. "I *love* cake!" She grabbed Elijah's hand and tugged him energetically inside the house.

Elijah chuckled and stepped inside the foyer.

Carter did his best to ignore the way Elijah's low laughter had just danced down his spine. "Wait. You're a chef?"

Elijah nodded. "A pastry chef. Although I'm pretty good at cooking meals too." His tone had turned strangely defensive.

Carter winced. "I'm sorry, I didn't mean that in a disparaging way. I've never met a chef who's so—" He stopped and swallowed his words before glancing at Maisie.

She was looking impatiently from Elijah to Carter and back again. "Does that mean Elijah will stay and make us hot dogs?"

"We were coming over to invite you for dinner," Carter explained at Elijah's bewildered look. He scratched his head with a chagrined grimace. "Although, now that I know you're a chef, I'd be pretty embarrassed to make anything for you."

Elijah blinked before bursting out laughing. "You can't be that bad."

This time, Carter's stomach did more than just flutter. It practically flipflopped, sending a flash of desire through him. He cursed his treacherous libido.

Shit. Is this because I haven't had sex in over a month? Or is it because it's him?

In the end, Elijah stayed and helped with dinner. From the enthusiastic noises Maisie made as she tucked into her meal, Elijah's assistance had apparently transformed Carter's mac and cheese into something deserving some kind of culinary award.

The cupcakes were the highlight of the night. Both Maisie and Carter practically groaned when they took their first bite of the delicious frosting and the fluffy, buttery sponge beneath.

"These are to die for," Carter murmured a while later. He licked his lips and eyed the box guiltily. There was only one cupcake left.

Elijah grinned around his cup of coffee. "I don't think Maisie can eat anymore and I'm quite full. You have it."

Carter sighed and patted his washboard stomach. "My personal trainer would kill me if he could see me right now."

Elijah raised an eyebrow. "You have a personal trainer?"

Oops.

"I, er, had one for a while," Carter replied evasively.

Elijah thankfully didn't pursue the matter further, although he did look at Carter pensively from time to time.

"Can Elijah read me a story again?" Maisie asked hesitantly when Elijah got ready to leave.

Carter looked anxiously at Elijah.

Elijah's mouth tilted in a gentle smile. "Sure."

This time, Maisie listened to the entire story, her eyes wide and bright. And at the end, she begged Elijah to tell it to her again. He obliged her without a protest. In that moment, Carter was willing to grant Elijah just about anything he wanted. Because the way Maisie's face lit up at Elijah's acquiescence was the sweetest thing in the world. She even joined in at one point, her voice growing in confidence as she and Elijah repeated the tale of the little girl who opened a bakery and ate too much cake.

"Elijah has to go home now, sweetheart," Carter said quietly when the story ended.

Maisie nodded, her eyes sleepy. "'kay."

Carter tucked her in and turned her night light on. Elijah was following him to the door when he made a surprised sound and stopped suddenly. Carter turned.

Maisie had bolted out of her bed and was squeezing Elijah's leg.

"Thank you for reading to me," she mumbled shyly. "And for the cakes."

She ran back to her bed, her face bright red, and hid under the covers.

Carter almost chuckled at Elijah's shocked expression.

"She really likes you," he said lightly after they exited the room.

"I can see that," Elijah said, his voice strangely quiet.

Mortification filled Carter when he registered Elijah's troubled expression. "I'm sorry if she was too forward. I'll tell her to hold back—"

"No." Elijah shook his head vigorously. "It's not that. I'm just—" He faltered and rubbed the back of his neck, clearly embarrassed. "I really like Maisie too. She is the sweetest kid I've ever met. It just breaks my heart she had to go through so much at such a young age." Something very much like admiration danced across his face. "She's lucky to have you, Carter."

Carter swallowed. Bar his close friends, this was the first time someone has said something like this to him in all the weeks since Louise and Mark's deaths. "Thank you." He hesitated. "It hasn't been easy. I still feel like I'm failing her most days."

They headed down the stairs.

"Look at it this way," Elijah said when they reached the front porch. "Most single men would never consider taking on a child on their own. If they did, they would rely heavily on their family for help. From what I've seen, you're on your own and you're doing everything you can for Maisie." He turned to Carter, a tiny frown wrinkling his brow. "You should give yourself some credit for that."

It was at that point that Carter realized he very much wanted to kiss Elijah. His gaze dropped unbidden to Elijah's lips.

"Oh. There's a bit of frosting on your—" He reached out unconsciously and wiped at the pale blue speck of colored sugar and cream at the corner of Elijah's mouth with his thumb.

Elijah froze, his lips parting slightly on a surprised inhale.

Carter went still.

Electricity filled the air between them, heat flashing between their skin where he touched Elijah. This time, Carter did not mistake the desire he glimpsed deep in the brown eyes opposite him. He took a step toward Elijah.

Elijah startled and backed away, breaking contact.

Carter slowly lowered his hand to his side, surprise by the acute disappointment shooting through him.

"I—" Elijah started. He faltered, red flags blooming on his cheekbones. "Goodnight." He turned and rushed down the steps.

Carter watched as Elijah disappeared into the night, no longer able to deny what it was he was feeling.

He was attracted to Elijah.

CHAPTER SEVEN

"Wait." Sam raised a hand, her eyes narrowing accusingly. "So, you've become friends with the neighbors who were keeping you up? And it's a hot, single guy raising his newly orphaned niece? And they're coming to visit?!"

Elijah grimaced. "I never said he was hot. And yeah, Maisie wanted to see the bakery."

"Oh, he's hot all right," Sam stated adamantly. "I can tell from the way your ears just turned red." She pointed a finger. "That, and the fact that you poured vanilla essence in that bowl instead of rose."

Elijah stared into the cake mix. "Damn it."

Sam crossed her arms and leaned against the table while Elijah grabbed another bowl and started over again. "So, you guys are close now?"

Elijah paused, measuring cup poised above the container of flour. "Kinda."

It had been ten days since he'd stormed into Carter's house and discovered the circumstances behind Maisie's crying fits. They'd spent most of their evenings together since, Elijah going over whenever he came home from work.

He'd asked the local library for French children's story books to read to Maisie a few days ago and they'd promised to call him when the items arrived. Elijah knew the surprise would please the little girl and make Carter happy too. His pulse leapt slightly when he thought of Maisie's uncle.

There hadn't been a repeat of the incident of the second night, when he could have sworn Carter had been about to kiss him on his porch. Half of him had been relieved that the simmering sexual tension that had flared between them had not manifested itself since, while the other half had been strangely disappointed.

Elijah berated himself silently. He had chosen to put his attraction to Carter down to the fact that he hadn't had sex for several months and was determined to stick to his decision to not get involved with his dangerously handsome neighbor.

No good can come out of it. And it will only hurt Maisie's feelings if things get awkward between us. Besides, I don't think he's gay.

Elijah's cell dinged with an incoming message, distracting him from his muddled thoughts. He wiped his hands on a towel and checked his phone.

"What is it?" Sam said.

"It's Carter." Elijah shot her a puzzled glance. "He's near the shop. He's asking if he and Maisie can come to the back door."

"Wait." Sam stared. "Did you say 'Carter'?"

৯৯

CARTER CURSED HIMSELF SILENTLY WHERE HE LOITERED at the mouth of the alleyway.

"Uncle Carter?" Maisie said where she stood holding his hand, her tone hesitant.

"It's okay, sweetheart."

Carter studied the line in front of *La Petite Bouche Gourmande* with a frown. He should have known Elijah's bakery would be hugely popular. He just hadn't expected for there to be an actual lineup of people outside the place.

Maisie's fingers clenched around his. "Is it the papazzi? Should we go home?"

Carter would have chuckled at the way she butchered the word had it not been for the fact that she was clinging to him, her anxiety plain to see.

"No," he said in a reassuring voice, "it isn't reporters." His phone vibrated in his hand. He looked at the text on the screen and heaved a sigh. "Come on, let's go this way."

He put his sunglasses on, tucked his Lakers cap down low, and headed across the road with Maisie. They entered a side alley, walked around to the back, crossed another lane, and finally reached the rear of Elijah's store. Carter looked up and down the passage to make sure no one was around, before knocking on the fire door.

It was opened almost immediately by Elijah.

"No, Sam, I never asked for his surname," the pastry chef was saying to someone over his shoulder, his tone clearly exasperated. "I seriously doubt he's a movie star. I'm sure there's a simple explanation for why he wanted to come this way."

Carter barely had time to register how sexy Elijah looked in his white chef uniform before his stomach sank at his words.

Uh-oh.

Elijah turned, his mouth tilting in a rueful smile as he looked at Carter and Maisie.

"Hey, you two. Come on in."

Carter hesitated. Maisie tugged on his hand, her eyes shining with excitement as she peered around Elijah's legs into a gaily decorated kitchen. He clenched his jaw and entered the building with the little girl.

A gasp reached him. Carter gazed warily at the young woman with the vibrant pink and blue hair gaping at him from across the room.

"Holy shit. It *is* you!"

⸙

ELIJAH FROWNED AT SAM.

"Er, language, please?" He indicated Maisie with a grimace.

His manager ignored him for a moment, her round eyes locked on the man who had just walked through the back door. She glanced apologetically at Maisie.

"I'm sorry, sweetie." Sam pointed at Carter. "*That* is

Carter Wilson." She stared at Elijah. "How the hell did you not recognize him?!"

Elijah blinked. The name was vaguely familiar. He turned to the man who stood watching them with a contrite expression. "Carter?"

Carter sighed. He took his sunglasses and cap off and ran a hand through his hair. "I'm sorry. I didn't mean to hide the truth from you. I just—" He faltered, his tone turning defensive as he met Elijah's shocked gaze. "I just liked the fact that you didn't know who I was and you treated me like I was a normal person."

Elijah's stomach plummeted. "Wait. Are you really some kind of hot shot movie star?"

"Try the highest grossing actor in all of Hollywood right now," Sam scoffed. "His movies are all blockbusters." She waved a hand at Elijah, a vexed look on her face. "You would know that, of course, if you hadn't been living under a rock."

The swing door to the shop opened a fraction. Daisy poked her head through the gap. "Er, Sam, I'm going to need some help out *holy crap, it's Carter Wilson!*"

Someone sucked in air audibly somewhere behind Daisy.

"What?! Did you just say Carter Wilson is here?!" a woman screeched.

"Excuse us." Sam smiled brightly and pushed Daisy out into the front of the shop before following her. She popped her head back in. "Don't anybody go anywhere. I'm gonna need details."

Carter rubbed a hand down his face as the door swung closed behind her. "I'm really sorry about this."

Elijah swallowed. He didn't know what to say.

"Uncle Carter?" Maisie mumbled.

Elijah almost cursed when he looked down and registered the little girl's troubled expression where she stood hugging Carter's leg.

"It's okay, Maisie." Elijah dropped down on his haunches and extended a hand to her. "How about I show you around the kitchen and we make some cupcakes?"

Maisie's face cleared. She nodded and took his hand.

CHAPTER EIGHT

CARTER TOOK A COUPLE OF BEERS OUT OF THE refrigerator and headed out onto his rear porch. Elijah was sitting on the swing and gazing pensively out at the dark forest beyond the back yard.

"Here you go." Carter handed a can to Elijah.

"Thanks," Elijah murmured.

Carter had just put Maisie to bed. Much to his relief, Elijah had agreed to stay back so they could talk. He took the spot next to Elijah.

"Again, I'm sorry about what happened at the bakery."

Elijah frowned at him faintly before popping his drink open. "To be honest, I'm still upset with you. You lied by omission."

Guilt twisted Carter's stomach.

"But I can also see why you did it," Elijah added quietly. He took a swig of his beer.

"You do?"

Elijah swallowed and grimaced. "You have Maisie to

look after. The last thing she needs right now are curious people gawking at you and butting into your lives."

Carter was silent for a moment. "I have to say, I was surprised when you didn't recognize me."

Elijah arched an eyebrow.

"I'm not saying that out of vanity," Carter continued hastily. "It's just—well, I guess you're not a movie fan, huh?" He rubbed the back of his head and directed an awkward smile at Elijah.

Elijah's lips twitched. "I prefer the classics. And my life as a chef means I don't have a lot of spare time. Although, Sam did berate me heavily for not knowing you were one of the 'Terrible Seven.'"

Carter flushed slightly. "Oh. She told you about that too, did she?"

Elijah leaned against the backrest, his expression amused. "Is it true that you guys spray painted the principal's car red when you were in middle school?"

Carter sighed and took a sip of his beer. "Yeah."

"What about the story of how you brought a prized bull in the girls' locker room in high school?"

Carter closed his eyes briefly as he recollected that particular incident. "That one is true too. Drake's uncle has a farm not far from here."

Elijah grinned. "I wish I'd been there to see it."

"Getting that brute into the building wasn't easy," Carter mumbled. "It almost gored me twice."

Elijah chuckled. The sound made Carter's pulse speed up.

They chatted companionably while they drank

their beers, Carter telling Elijah how he'd gone to L.A. to become an actor and Elijah talking about his grandmother and the reason he'd become a pastry chef. Carter's eyes widened when Elijah mentioned the name of the restaurant he'd worked at before moving back to Twilight Falls.

"You're kidding me? That's one of the most famous places to eat at in Paris!"

Although Elijah shrugged nonchalantly, Carter could tell he was pleased by the compliment from the way his ears reddened slightly.

"No wonder your bakery is already such a success," Carter said admiringly. "There is also, well—" He indicated Elijah's face and figure with a vague motion of his hand.

Elijah looked at him, puzzled. "What?"

Carter stared. *He really doesn't know, does he?*

"You're hot," he blurted out.

Elijah blinked. To Carter's delight, he flushed a delectable shade of pink.

"Hmm, I think that description fits you better," Elijah mumbled.

Carter grinned. "Okay, how about we agree that we're *both* shamefully sexy?"

Elijah shook his head and laughed. "You sure are cocky, aren't you?"

Goosebumps broke out on Carter's arms at the sound of Elijah's laughter. The amusement faded from Elijah's face when he registered Carter's intense stare.

Heat sparked between them.

Elijah's pupils dilated at the sexual tension suddenly

thrumming the air. He swallowed and rose to his feet. "I should head home."

Carter followed Elijah into the kitchen and caught up with him at the island.

"Are you gay?" he said quietly.

Elijah stilled at the question, his back to Carter. "Yes, I am." He put his empty can down on the marble top and turned, his expression somewhat defiant as he studied Carter. "But you aren't."

Carter's heart thudded rapidly at Elijah's confession. "No, I'm not."

Something that looked a lot like disappointment flitted in Elijah's eyes.

Carter wondered if he would come to regret what he was about to say next.

"I'm bi."

Elijah froze, surprise widening his eyes. "What?"

Carter took a step toward him. This time, Elijah held his ground.

Elijah's breath hitched slightly when Carter placed his hands on the island on either side of him, trapping him in. He tilted his head and stared unblinkingly at Carter, color staining his cheekbones. Carter had a couple of inches on him height wise.

"I said I'm bisexual," Carter said in a low voice, his gaze locked on Elijah's.

He leaned in.

Elijah stopped breathing. Carter's cock throbbed when he saw the pulse beating wildly at the base of Elijah's throat.

"Tell me if you don't want this," Carter said huskily.

Elijah let out a shaky breath. He swayed slightly toward Carter.

That was all it took for Carter to give in to the desire swarming his blood and kiss Elijah.

❧

ELIJAH'S HEART THUNDERED AGAINST HIS RIBS AT THE first touch of Carter's lips.

He couldn't believe that this was happening. That he was standing in the kitchen of a world famous movie star and being kissed by him. Except Carter wasn't just a movie star. He was an uncle to a little girl who desperately needed his love. And he was a man who'd embraced the difficult task of raising a child on his own.

He was also the one person Elijah hadn't been able to get out of his mind for the last ten days.

Elijah's eyes fluttered close at Carter's gentle kiss. Carter was exploring his mouth lazily, as if he wanted to take his time and commit the shape of his lips to memory. Elijah sighed and looped his arms languidly around Carter's neck.

It was as if he'd ignited a fuse somewhere inside Carter with that simple gesture.

Elijah gasped when Carter moved his hands to his waist and pressed his body into him, a low groan rumbling from his throat. He probed Elijah's lips commandingly with his hot tongue.

Heat exploded inside Elijah when Carter entered his mouth. He moaned, his cock stiffening behind the zipper of his jeans as Carter wrapped his tongue around his, tugging and caressing his trembling flesh. Carter ran his hands down Elijah's hips before clasping his ass firmly and pulling him closer. Elijah shuddered when he felt Carter's erection pressing against his own hard flesh.

Oh God.

This kiss was as fierce as the sun. And he was drowning in it.

Carter finally let go of Elijah's mouth. He inhaled raggedly and pressed his forehead against Elijah's. They looked dazedly at each other in the fraught silence, their breaths coming hard and fast, their faces flushed.

"I've been dying to do that since the day I met you," Carter whispered.

Elijah bit his lip at Carter's heartfelt confession. Carter's gaze dropped to Elijah's mouth. He raised a hand and ran a thumb over where Elijah's top teeth dug into the plump, moist flesh.

"Don't," Carter murmured. "You'll leave a mark."

Elijah shuddered at Carter's sensual touch. He unconsciously licked his lips.

Carter's eyes flared when Elijah's tongue connected with his finger.

"Are you trying to kill me?" Carter groaned. "Because, trust me, the only thing holding me back from taking you upstairs and making love to you right now is the fact that I know it's way too early for us to do that." He paused and caressed Elijah's lip once more, his expression softening. "For *you* to do that.

Something tells me you're not a one-night stand kinda guy."

Elijah swallowed, blood pounding in his veins. "Are you?"

Carter blinked, as if the question surprised him. Elijah's heart sank when he saw the answer in Carter's eyes.

"I'm not going to lie to you," Carter said quietly. "I don't normally do relationships."

Dismay filled Elijah at Carter's words.

Carter stroked his knuckles gently down Elijah's cheek. "But this," he murmured, his gaze shining so brightly it threatened to scorch Elijah, "this feeling. It's different. *You're* different."

Elijah shivered and closed his eyes briefly against Carter's heated stare.

Is he being honest? Or is he just saying that because he wants to sleep with me?

"So I want to take things easy." Carter let go of Elijah and took a step back.

Elijah almost protested at the move, feeling oddly bereft all of a sudden.

"I want to get to know you better," Carter stated in a serious voice. "And I want you to get to know me too. The real me."

CHAPTER NINE

Carter looked at her blankly where they sat on her back porch steps. "What do you mean?"

A high-pitched giggle distracted him. His gaze shifted to where Maisie played in a paddling pool with Wyatt in the yard below, her face beaming as she splashed him.

It was Saturday and Elijah was still working at the bakery. The weather had turned hot and Carter had accepted Izzy and Wyatt's invitation to come over for the afternoon.

Izzy glanced at the little girl. "Both of you seem more relaxed," she said quietly. "And I've never seen Maisie like this. Is she still having nightmares?"

Carter shook his head, the relief he'd experienced over the last two weeks washing over him once more. "No. She hasn't had them in a while now."

Izzy's face brightened. "That's great! So the new therapist is working out?"

Carter shrugged evasively. "Yeah. That and other things."

Affection warmed his heart as he studied his niece. Maisie was a different child to the one he'd brought to Twilight Falls. And he knew he had Elijah to thank for that. It was obvious how much Maisie adored the chef from the way she acted around him and talked about him nonstop when he wasn't around. And he knew Elijah cherished Maisie just as much.

Carter's mouth curved faintly when he recalled Maisie's overjoyed face last night, when Elijah brought over a stack of French bedtime stories he'd ordered from the library to read to her. Carter had even reluctantly participated when Maisie begged him to tell him one of the stories and fake pouted when Elijah and Maisie teased him for his terrible accent.

"What's that smile for?" Izzy said quizzically.

Carter cursed internally. Izzy had an unerringly ability to be right on target when it came to her friends' love lives. It was her meddling that had resulted in Alex and Finn's paths crossing and Carter strongly suspected she'd engineered their romance to an extent.

The doorbell rang, saving him from further inquisition. Izzy rose and went inside the house. She returned shortly, her voice animated as she chatted to the figures in her wake.

"Look who decided to drop by," Izzy said with a grin. "I told them you and Maisie were coming over. Alex and Finn couldn't make it. They're in San Diego."

Carter smiled at the two men who walked out onto the porch after Izzy. "Hey."

"Hey yourself," Drake said. Tristan nodded a hello and dropped down on the step next to Carter.

"Isn't Hunter with you?" Carter said.

"He said he had to pick something up." Drake leaned his elbows on the railing and gazed thoughtfully to where Wyatt and Maisie played in the water. "This sure is different from what I'd thought it would be."

"I was just saying that," Izzy said.

"Maisie looks happy," Tristan murmured.

Carter nodded, emotion flooding his chest. He couldn't feel more content than he did right now, sitting in the sun in his friends' backyard, surrounded by his favorite people in the world. Elijah's face drifted before his eyes.

This day would be perfect if he were here too.

He and Elijah hadn't kissed since that night in his kitchen four days ago, Carter keeping true to his promise that he wouldn't rush their relationship. He suppressed a wry grimace at that thought.

Relationship, huh? I never thought the day would come when I would ever use that word with regards to myself.

Carter was conscious of the fact that what he was feeling for Elijah was more than sexual attraction. He found Elijah captivating not just because of his looks, but because of his personality and his warm, generous nature. Elijah had a heart big enough to heal both Carter and Maisie and he'd been doing so unconsciously since the day he first stormed inside their home, completely unaware of the profound effect his kind smiles and words had had on them.

Carter knew that his time in L.A. had made him

jaded. The people he hung out with in Hollywood were more interested in his fame and money than in who he was as a person. As such, he tended to mistrust most strangers.

Yet, he had never felt that way around Elijah. He was comfortable with him, as comfortable as he was with the friends he'd grown up with. And that said a lot about his growing emotions for the sexy pastry chef.

Hunter arrived just as the sun started to dip behind the trees hedging Izzy and Wyatt's back yard. Carter wrapped Maisie in a towel before taking her inside the house, Wyatt staying back to dismantle the paddling pool. Maisie leaned her head tiredly against Carter's shoulder and yawned. Carter smiled faintly; he suspected she wouldn't need a bedtime story to fall asleep that night. He slowed and stopped when he saw the cream and duck egg blue box on Izzy and Wyatt's kitchen table.

Damn.

"You have *got* to taste these cupcakes!" Hunter was gushing as he took out serving plates and dessert forks from Izzy and Wyatt's cabinets and drawers. "They are the most divine things I have ever put in my mouth. And I have put *many* divine things in my mouth."

Izzy tapped him sharply on the back of his head. "There is a child present."

Hunter glanced guiltily at Maisie and Carter. "Sorry."

"Isn't that from the new bakery that just opened up?" Tristan said as Hunter opened the box. "The one that always has a line outside?"

Hunter nodded. "Yup. Apparently, the guy who runs it was born in Twilight Falls and went to Paris to train to be a pastry chef. I had to order these suckers four days in advance, their waiting list is so long."

Drake read out the name on the business card taped to the lid of the box. *"La Petite Bouche Gourmande."*

Maisie lifted her head from Carter's shoulder and rubbed her eyes drowsily.

"Your French is terrible," Izzy admonished. "That's not how you say it. It's—"

"La Petite Bouche Gourmande." Maisie said in perfect French. "Uncle Carter, look. It's Uncle Elijah's cakes."

Carter tried not to squirm when he became the focus of a battery of stares.

Izzy raised an eyebrow. "Elijah?"

Maisie nodded vigorously. "That's Elijah's shop. He makes the best cakes in the world. And he reads me bedtime stories every night." She paused and looked guiltily at Carter. "Uncle Carter reads to me too."

The stares became laser-like.

"Really?" Hunter said with a slow smile. "Rumor has it this Elijah is a hunk."

"What's a hunk?" Maisie asked, puzzled.

Carter muttered something rude under his breath. Tristan sighed.

Hunter grinned, came around the table, and tapped a gentle finger on the tip of Maisie's nose. "It's a beautiful person that you like spending time with."

Maisie's eyes rounded. "Oh." She paused. "Uncle Elijah is definitely that." She blushed before stating in a voice brimming with confidence. "I'm gonna marry Uncle Elijah when I'm all grown up."

Carter blinked at his niece, more than a little bit shocked.

Izzy chuckled. "Oh my."

"What?" Carter said defensively.

"You should wipe that green-eyed look from your face." Hunter's eyes twinkled teasingly. "It's most unbecoming."

Carter opened and closed his mouth soundlessly in the face of his friends' amused expressions.

"You can marry Uncle Elijah too," Maisie told Carter hesitantly. "I don't mind sharing."

CHAPTER TEN

Elijah pulled into his driveway, turned the Citroën's engine off, and stepped out of the car. He glanced across the road. Bar the porch lights, Carter and Maisie's home was dark.

Maybe they've gone to see one of Carter's friends.

Elijah went inside his house and had just taken a bottle of water out of the fridge when the low rumble of a car outside reached his ears. He stiffened slightly when he recognized the sound of Carter's Maserati.

Four days had passed since he and Carter had shared their first kiss. Carter had kept his promise and hadn't touched him once since. Elijah should have been relieved by this. Except he wasn't.

He'd looked up Carter since he found out his new neighbor was a famous movie star. What he'd discovered was that the man wasn't just one of the highest grossing actors in the world right now, but he was also the tabloids' favorite target.

Even though Carter had made no secret of the fact

that he preferred to engage in no-strings-attached sex to Elijah, it was clear the media loved portraying the actor as some kind of villainous cad who had left a trail of broken hearts all over Hollywood. Elijah knew Carter had more than likely gotten used to being in the constant glare of the media's attention and to the sensationalist tales going around about him, since it came with the territory of his chosen career. Still, the lies they contained had upset Elijah.

The lurid accounts he had read were in sharp contrast to the man he'd gotten to know over the last two weeks.

They obviously don't know the real Carter Wilson.

Carter's words the night they'd kissed rose in Elijah's mind at that thought. He wondered if any of Carter's previous lovers had looked beyond the facade of the famous Hollywood movie star to the man beneath.

The third thing that had jumped out at Elijah was that he hadn't seen any mention of the actor being linked to another man in a romantic sense. Which meant his confession to Elijah about his bisexuality was a closely guarded secret.

The fact that Carter had chosen to confide in him humbled Elijah like little else could. It also told him just how much Carter had come to respect and trust him in the short time they'd known each other.

Elijah's cell buzzed in the back pocket of his jeans. He took it out and looked at the text that had come through.

Carter: Want to come over for a beer?

Elijah hesitated before replying.

Elijah: Sure. Give me ten minutes. Beer's on me.

Elijah headed across the road with a six-pack a short while later, his hair still wet from the shower he'd just taken. Carter opened the front door just as he reached the porch.

"Hey." Carter's face relaxed in a warm smile.

Elijah's pulse jumped. Carter had also taken a shower and smelled divine. Not only that, he looked positively sinful as he stood barefoot in dark sweatpants and a gray T-shirt. Elijah swallowed the sudden nervous lump in his throat and stepped inside the foyer.

"Is Maisie still up?"

"She was out like a light by the time we got home," Carter said ruefully, closing the door. "We were at Izzy and Wyatt's this afternoon. I didn't have the heart to wake her up for a bedtime story. She'll be sorry she missed you."

They headed through the house and out to the back porch.

A tired sigh left Elijah as they settled on the swing. He popped the lid on his can and took a sip of his beer.

"Busy day?" Carter asked lightly, opening his own drink.

Elijah nodded. "Yeah. I didn't think we'd still be this hectic after the opening. We're even taking orders from out of town. At this rate, I'm gonna need to hire a sous-chef."

Carter grinned. "That's great news." His smile faded

slightly. "By the way, my friends may have discovered our connection. Don't be surprised if they turn up at some point to check you out."

Elijah stared at him, surprised. "What do you mean?"

"Hunter picked up cupcakes from your shop today," Carter replied with an awkward look. "Maisie saw the box and spilled the beans about you coming over every night."

Elijah's heart thumped hard against his ribs at Carter's words. "Do your friends know about—?" He stopped, his gaze dropping briefly to Carter's mouth.

Carter's expression sobered. "About our kiss and the fact that we're dating? No."

Elijah blinked. "We're dating?"

Carter's face fell. "Well, yeah."

He looked so crestfallen, Elijah couldn't help but chuckle. "Sorry, I thought we were still at the stage of testing things out." He arched an eyebrow. "Besides, you haven't officially asked me out."

Carter relaxed at his teasing tone. "Guess I haven't, huh?" He cleared his throat. "Elijah Davis, will you go out with me?"

Elijah studied him for a moment before shrugging. "I suppose I could."

Carter's eyes rounded comically. Elijah burst out laughing.

"You really should stop teasing me," Carter grumbled. "By the way, I fear I may have a competitor for your attention."

"What do you mean?"

Carter sighed. "Maisie said she wants to marry you."

Elijah choked and spewed out the mouthful of beer he'd just taken.

Carter chuckled and rose to his feet while Elijah flicked beer off his T-shirt and jeans. "I thought you might take it that way. Wait, let me grab something to dry you up."

He went inside the house and came back out with a kitchen towel.

"I'm okay," Elijah protested when Carter sat next to him and started dabbing at his chest and thighs.

Butterflies filled Elijah's stomach at the feel of Carter's hands on his body. He held his breath and avoided Carter's gaze, desperate not to show the other man how much his closeness was affecting him. Heat flashed through his veins when Carter's fingers accidentally brushed across his left nipple.

Elijah couldn't help the shiver that raced through him.

Carter stilled, his palm resting lightly on Elijah's chest. "Your heart's beating mighty fast," he said quietly.

"Is it?" Elijah mumbled. He raised his chin and finally met Carter's stare. His breath caught.

Carter's eyes blazed with desire and a healthy dose of frustration.

"Why are you hesitating?"

The words left Elijah before he could help himself. He bit his lip, conscious he'd just expressed his exasperation about Carter not making a move on him for the past few days.

Taut silence fell between them.

"Because I respect you," Carter finally admitted, a muscle dancing in his jawline. "I don't want this to just be about sex, like my other affairs."

CHAPTER ELEVEN

"And I don't want you to hold back either." Elijah frowned. "I'm not going to run away if you touch me, Carter."

Carter groaned at Elijah's words. Elijah startled when Carter dropped his head against his shoulder.

"You have no idea the filthy things that I want to do to you," Carter admitted in a low voice, his heart slamming against his ribcage. "*With* you."

"I'm not a prude. And, to be honest, I've been feeling pretty frustrated too."

Carter froze before raising his head and staring at Elijah.

What he read in the dark eyes opposite him had blood rushing to his head.

Carter held Elijah's gaze and stroked a thumb gently across his mouth. Elijah inhaled sharply and unconsciously licked his lips.

The flick of his hot tongue against Carter's finger pad made Carter's cock harden.

Carter trailed his fingers down Elijah's throat and chest. Elijah closed his eyes and arched sensuously into Carter's touch. His growing arousal did not escape Carter's attention.

"Jesus, you're hot." Carter's voice grew rough when he registered the erection straining Elijah's jeans. "Can I really touch you?"

"You're already touching me," Elijah breathed.

Carter stroked Elijah's left nipple.

Elijah shuddered. "Damn. That feels good!" He opened his eyes, clasped Carter's face in his hands, and took his mouth in a passionate kiss.

Carter blinked, a little stunned. Then his hands were on Elijah's face and in his hair, his grip almost punishing. He slipped his tongue past Elijah's hot, hungry lips and invaded his mouth. Elijah trembled when Carter entwined their flesh in a bold, titillating dance.

Carter lowered his hands to Elijah's chest and rubbed his hard nipples through his T-shirt. Elijah moaned and twitched. Carter's dick did press-ups in his sweatpants at the sexy sound. He skimmed a hand down Elijah's six-pack and tense belly before stroking the back of his fingers lightly across Elijah's raging erection.

Elijah sucked in air and grabbed Carter's shoulders, his hips punching up reflexively into Carter's touch. The erotic move had Carter wrenching his mouth jerkily from Elijah's and dropping to his knees in front of him.

Elijah's eyes widened in surprise. He flushed as

Carter frantically unbuckled his jeans and drew his zipper down. A low groan left him when his cock sprung free seconds later.

"Beautiful." Carter's pulse raced as he studied Elijah's glistening, engorged flesh. He traced the veins covering Elijah's shaft with a finger before swiping at the precum oozing out of the tip with his thumb. "Every goddamn inch of you is beautiful."

Elijah's breath hitched. "Carter!"

Carter closed a hand around Elijah's erection and gave him exactly what he was begging for, his touch firm as he started stroking him. A low hum escaped Elijah. He gripped the edge of the swing with white-knuckled fingers and opened his thighs wider.

Lust swirled through Carter at Elijah's pleasure-flushed face and straining body. His gaze dropped to the hard nubs poking Elijah's T-shirt.

Carter took hold of the hem and pushed the material up. He nearly cursed when he exposed a bewitching expanse of toned muscles and honey-colored skin dusted with fine, downy hair. His gaze arrowed in on Elijah's taut nipples.

"I knew they'd be brown. Like chocolate." Carter leaned in and closed his mouth hungrily on Elijah's left nipple, eager to taste the stiff, cocoa-colored nub. His other hand found Elijah's right nipple and pinched and twisted the hard flesh gently.

Elijah closed his eyes and worked his fingers in Carter's hair. His head dropped against the backrest as he gave in to pleasure, his hips rolling his shaft sensuously through Carter's skillful grip. Every tug and suck of Carter's clever fingers and mouth on his nipples had him shivering and moaning, heightening Carter's own arousal. Carter could tell from the way Elijah kept biting his lip that he was trying hard to keep his voice down.

The way Elijah's balls tightened and his movements became jerky a moment later told Carter he was close to climaxing. Elijah looked down and groaned when he met Carter's blazing stare, his cheekbones and ears rosy with color.

"Let go!" Elijah wrapped a hand around Carter's where the latter stroked his dick. "I'm gonna come!"

Carter's fingers tightened on Elijah's pulsing flesh. "Then come," he growled in a commanding voice. He closed his teeth on Elijah's left nipple, tugged on the swollen nub, and circled his thumb on the head of Elijah's cock, his eyes still holding Elijah's.

Air locked in Elijah's throat as he exploded in Carter's hand. He shut his eyes tight, his body stiffening like a bow. Shudders shook him as he convulsed on the swing, the faint sound of the hinges creaking a lewd soundtrack to the sultry gasps and groans escaping his lips.

Blood pounded in Carter's ears when Elijah finally slumped onto the seat, his chest heaving and his limbs trembling in the aftermath of his orgasm.

So goddamn sexy.

Elijah opened his eyes in time to see Carter swipe his tongue lazily across his cum-slick thumb.

Carter shot him a teasing smile. "Sweet."

Elijah flushed at the filthy move. His gaze dropped

to the erection tenting Carter's sweatpants. "Want some help with that?"

Carter grimaced and shook his head. "If you touch me right now, I'll go off like a bomb. Why don't you relax and enjoy the show?" He sat back on his heels, pushed his pants down his hips, and freed his swollen cock.

Surprise widened Elijah's eyes. He swallowed when he saw the thick shaft sprouting from Carter's trimmed pubes.

Carter started stroking himself, his movements slick with Elijah's cum, his gaze locked on the man opposite him.

This right here, him pleasuring himself openly in front of Elijah as if he were in the privacy of his own bedroom, was a pure demonstration of just how much of a sexual creature he truly was. From Elijah's enraptured expression and the fact that he couldn't look away, he found the act just as thrilling.

Sweat pearled Carter's upper lip as he rubbed his leaking cock briskly, his pace accelerating and his mouth opening on rough pants, bolts of pure electricity shooting through him. The feel of Elijah's eyes on him heightened the sinful sensation of his own hand on his painfully hard cock ten-fold.

The first ripple of Carter's climax danced down his spine and through his thighs. It pooled deep inside his belly, a slow building inferno that matched his rising heartbeat and his ragged breathing.

Elijah dug his nails into his palms, clearly forcing himself not to touch Carter like he was dying to.

Carter's gaze dropped to Elijah's white knuckles. "Elijah."

The sultry sound of his name on Carter's lips was Elijah's undoing. He cursed, gripped Carter's face, and kissed him hard.

Their harsh breaths mingled and their tongues clashed as Carter's climax bore down on him. Then he was rising on his knees and grunting and groaning, his body rigid with orgasmic tension, his cock pulsing jet after jet of thick cum onto his fingers as he came violently at Elijah's feet.

CHAPTER TWELVE

"Sweet Jesus," Sam muttered. "I can literally see ovaries exploding out there."

Elijah looked up distractedly from where he brushed glazing over a tray of tarts. Sam was standing in the kitchen and poking her head out of a gap in the swing door that led to the shop.

"What's going on?"

Sam rolled her eyes at him over her shoulder. "Did you not hear me say we had some special guests turn up?"

Elijah raised an eyebrow. "Special how?" His pulse stuttered. He put down the brush, wiped his hands on a towel, and hurried over to the door. "Wait. Don't tell me Carter is out there!"

"You wish it were Carter," Sam said drily. "Jeez, Elijah, I don't think I've ever seen you move so fast."

Elijah ignored her teasing tone and peered over her head.

The bakery was packed. This was not unusual in

itself. What was unusual was the group of attractive men seated at a dainty table overlooking the street, looking as incongruous as a pack of wolves at a lambing party among the dozens of women crammed around them.

"Hottie number one on the left with the dark hair and gray eyes is Hunter Thomson," Sam murmured. "He owns the biggest sports apparel store in town. The guy next to him is Tristan Hart. He's a mechanic and luxury car and bike specialist. The blond is Alex Hancock, a lawyer. He's married to Finn West, our local artist extraordinaire. And finally, the rugged dreamboat with the blue eyes and brown hair, FYI the only man I would *ever* consider sleeping with, is Drake Jackson. He's one of the most sought-after builders this side of the San Bernardino Mountains." A sigh left her lips. "I never thought I would see half of the Terrible Seven sitting in our bakery, eating cake and drinking tea and coffee out of fine China. I feel we should do something to immortalize this moment."

"Like what?" Elijah murmured, trying his best to ignore the nervous tension coiling through him.

"I don't know, cover them in cream and lick them?" Sam suggested, waving a hand vaguely. "I bet people would pay a lot of money to see that."

Elijah frowned as he studied the men who seemed oblivious to the avid stares they were drawing. From what Carter had told him a couple of nights ago, Elijah suspected this was the unofficial "checking him out" visit.

Memories of what had happened between Carter

and him on Carter's back porch danced through Elijah's mind, like it had done countless times since that night. Heat flooded his face.

Did that really happen?

Elijah had spent the rest of that night and the one after that all hot and bothered, to the point he'd had to give himself several handjobs to calm his raging libido and get to sleep. He became conscious of Sam's curious glance as he gazed out at Carter's friends.

Well, as long as I stay in the kitchen, they won't see me. 'Cause if they do, I get the feeling they'll read my face like a book.

The bakery's front door opened on a sudden blast of fresh air.

"Oh God," Sam groaned. "That's Wyatt Batista. Holy crap, it's like all my Christmases just came at once."

Ethan stared at the tall, quiet-looking man with the green eyes and dark hair who'd just walked inside the shop. A woman with similar coloring came in behind him, her sparkling gaze sweeping the interior of the bakery curiously.

"Shit." Sam ducked back inside the kitchen, color rising in her cheekbones.

Elijah stared at her. "What's wrong?"

"Nothing," Sam mumbled.

A flash of intuition darted through Elijah as he observed the brunette who'd just joined the Terrible Seven. "She's pretty."

"Yeah, she is." Sam twisted a lock of hair between her fingers.

The nervous movement told Elijah he was bang on the money.

Sam had a crush on the brunette.

The woman called Daisy over with a dazzling smile. The waitress headed to the table that had become the focus of the bakery's attention, her gaze flicking nervously to the men gathered around the brunette. Her face fell as she listened to whatever the woman was saying to her. She shook her head.

Hunter Thomson murmured something before flashing a killer smile at the waitress. Daisy blinked and flushed.

"Uh-oh." Sam had squeezed her head past Elijah and was staring through the gap in the swing door once more. "I smell trouble."

Elijah stiffened when Daisy turned and came slowly toward the kitchen. His back pocket buzzed. He grabbed his cell.

Carter had just messaged him.

Carter: I'm on my way. Don't let those guys near you!

Elijah brought up the keyboard and started typing.

Elijah: How did you know they were here?!

Carter: Izzy texted and said the whole gang was headed to your bakery. Definitely stay away from that—

"'—Izzy,'" someone quoted in a low murmur behind Elijah. "'That Batista woman is a born trouble maker.' Well, he's coming off my Christmas list."

Elijah twisted on his heels. The brunette had followed Daisy and was peering over Elijah's shoulder at the text Carter had just sent. Sam stood round-eyed and pale-faced next to Elijah, too shocked to utter a word.

Elijah narrowed his eyes at Izzy Batista and put his phone away. "It's rude to read other people's messages. And customers aren't allowed back here."

"That's what I told her and the hot guy," Daisy murmured. "Then he smiled and my mind went kinda blank."

Izzy ignored Elijah's rebuke and grinned. "You must be Elijah." She extended a hand. "I'm Izzy."

Elijah hesitated before grudgingly shaking it. Izzy Batista had a magnetic charm that was hard to resist.

A low rumble outside the front of the bakery drew their attention.

A shiny black Harley-Davidson had just pulled up to the curb. A man dressed in biker clothes climbed off the motorcycle.

Elijah's stomach dropped when the rider removed his helmet and raked a hand through his thick, dark curls. "What the hell is he doing here?"

Sam blinked owlishly. Her jaw dropped. "Holy shit." She glanced at Elijah. "Is that who I think it is?!"

Izzy stared at the man who stood gazing at the bakery sign with a faint smile. "He looks kinda familiar."

The doorbell jangled as the guy came inside the shop. His blue gaze swept the interior before zeroing in on the swing door and the gap where Elijah stood between the three women.

"*Elijah, mon amour.*" He strode across the bakery, his

arms wide open and a bright smile lighting up his handsome face.

"Damn it," Elijah mumbled.

Sam opened and closed her mouth soundlessly.

"Who is that?" Izzy asked curiously while the women in the shop stared wide-eyed at the charismatic newcomer.

"That's Nicolas Perrault!" Sam squeaked. "The chef who won a Lebey Award three years in a row. Elijah was working at his restaurant in Paris!"

Nico stormed past Izzy and Daisy and swept Elijah up in his arms.

Elijah scowled. "What the—? Hey, Nico, stop—"

It was as far as he got before Nico took his mouth in an ardent kiss.

A shocked inhale reached Elijah's ears as he pushed Nico away. He turned.

Carter stood framed in the bakery's back door, the spare key Elijah had given him and his cell hanging limping from his hands, his expression stunned.

"Well, things sure just got interesting," Izzy said, deadpan.

CHAPTER THIRTEEN

"Carter, this is Nicolas Perrault, the owner of *Perrault*, in Paris," Elijah said stiffly. "Nico, this is Carter Wilson."

Carter kept his expression neutral as he studied the dark-haired man leaning casually against the counter as if he belonged in Elijah's kitchen.

"Ah. *Le fameux acteur*." Nico observed Carter with a faint smile. "How cliché."

Irritation surged through Carter at the man's mocking tone.

Elijah frowned at the French chef. "I don't know what you're doing here Nico, but if you're going to be rude, the back door is that way." He pointed a finger at the exit.

Nico gave Elijah a sickeningly indulgent look that made Carter want to punch him. "Come now, *mon amour*. I am here to claim you back. And it is obvious this man is my competition, *non?*"

Elijah flushed. "Claim me back?" he scoffed angrily.

"What am I, some kind of prize? And there is no competition. You and I were over a lifetime ago. I don't tolerate assholes who cheat on me."

Someone sucked in air.

The three men turned and stared at Izzy where she sat on a stool at the other end of the butcher's block.

"Don't mind me." Izzy pointed a fork at the cake she was eating and looked admiringly at Elijah. "By the way, this is to *die* for."

Elijah rubbed a hand across his eyes and sighed. "This is a private conversation."

"Yeah, don't you have somewhere to be?" Carter told Izzy coldly.

"Nope," Izzy replied succinctly.

The swing door opened. Wyatt strolled in. "Come on, let's go," he told his sister.

"But—but they're just getting to the good part! Besides, I haven't finished my cake!" Izzy protested.

Wyatt glanced at the three men before giving Izzy a stern look. "We can box the cake. The rest of the guys left a while ago."

He took her elbow and guided her out into the shop, Izzy cursing and clutching at her plate.

A fraught silence fell across the bakery's kitchen when the door swung shut behind the pair. Nervous tension hummed through Carter as he observed Elijah's furious expression. It was clear from Elijah's passionate reaction that he still harbored strong feelings toward the French chef, even if those feelings were borne of contempt.

Regret darkened Nico's eyes as he stared at Elijah.

"Six months is not a lifetime, *chéri*," he said quietly. "And I told you it was a mistake. One I will never make again."

A muscle twitched in Elijah's cheek. "It doesn't matter, Nico. Like I said, we're over."

Nico straightened and strolled over to Elijah. "Even if I were to tell you that I am considering opening a branch restaurant in L.A., like you always wanted?" He raised a finger to Elijah's chin and tilted his face up gently.

Surprise widened Elijah's pupils.

Carter clenched his fists. *That's it!*

He strode over to the two men and took a firm hold of Nico's wrist. "I would appreciate it if you kept your hands off my boyfriend."

Elijah blinked dazedly.

Nico slowly lowered his hand. Carter let go of the Frenchman's wrist.

"This is between Elijah and me," Nico told Carter coldly. "I would appreciate it if you would butt out."

"It's clear Elijah doesn't want you here." Carter glanced at Elijah, troubled by the stunned expression still pasted across the pastry chef's face. "Whatever it is you're up to, it's not going to work." He scowled at Nico.

Nico raised an eyebrow. "You make it sound as if I am skulking in the shadows, scheming an evil plot." He ignored Carter and looked at Elijah, his expression sobering. "I've taken a month's leave from *Perrault* to come scout out potential locations in L.A. I would like you to join me."

That made Elijah snap out of his daze. "You took a month's leave?!"

It was evident from Elijah's shocked tone that this was something out of the ordinary.

Nico smiled laconically. "I hired another sous-chef. That's how much this project means to me." He took a deep breath. "And you, Elijah. That's how much *you* mean to me, *mon amour*."

Elijah took a step back and shook his head, as if to deny the Frenchman's words. "No," he mumbled, pale-faced. "You're lying." He swallowed convulsively before fisting his hands and lifting his chin challengingly, his eyes hardening. "If you really cared for me, you wouldn't have cheated on me. I can't forgive you for what you did, Nico. You broke my heart." His voice trembled slightly. "And my trust."

Pain twisted through Carter at Elijah's tortured expression. "Elijah."

Elijah startled at the sound of his name. He turned and gazed at Carter as if he were seeing him for the first time. A bewildering sense of loss swamped Carter.

Resolve filled Elijah's eyes, as if he'd read Carter's agitated thoughts. To Carter's shock, Elijah reached over and took his hand.

"Carter and I are dating," Elijah told Nico firmly. "Nothing you do or say will come between that."

Carter's pulse hammered in his veins at Elijah's heartfelt admission. He linked his fingers with Elijah's.

Irritation flared in Nico's eyes as he gazed at their entwined hands. "We'll see about that." He frowned at

Carter. "Never underestimate the abilities of a Frenchman when it comes to affairs of the heart."

Carter narrowed his eyes. "And never underestimate the abilities of someone who may be falling in love for the first time in his life."

Elijah's fingers twitched around Carter's. He flushed as he looked at him, somewhat dumbfounded.

"Well, isn't that nice," Nico said tauntingly. "Now, where do you live Elijah? It's been a long day and I want to get some sleep."

Elijah's face went slack.

Carter stared suspiciously at the Frenchman. "Why do you want to know where he lives?"

"You are not staying over, Nico!" Elijah blurted out.

CHAPTER FOURTEEN

"I CAN'T BELIEVE YOU'RE LETTING HIM STAY OVER," Carter said darkly.

"I'm sorry," Elijah mumbled, contrite.

"You should have let him sleep in the gutter, like the dog that he is."

"I heard that." Nico narrowed his eyes at Carter where he stood making his world famous beef bourguignon at the cooking range in Carter's kitchen.

Maisie looked up from where she stood on a stepstool next to the French chef, her avid gaze switching from the divine-smelling casserole he was stirring, to Carter and Nico. A puzzled frown marred her brow. "Are you a dog, Nico?"

Nico's grim expression melted as he looked at the little girl. "*Non, ma chérie.* Your uncle was making a joke."

Relief danced across Maisie's face. "Nico can stay here if he doesn't have a place to sleep tonight," she told Carter hesitantly.

Elijah sighed at Carter's fairly mutinous expression. The fact that Nico had charmed the little girl within minutes of meeting her was not going down well with her uncle. Maisie oohing and aahing over the delicious meal Nico had made for them hardly helped matters later, though Carter showed willing when he grudgingly complimented the French chef on the food.

A bout of melancholy swirled through Elijah as he finished the last bite of the tender beef. It was his favorite dish from *Perrault* and the one that had earned Nico his first Michelin star. It was also one of the dishes Elijah used to ask Nico to make for him on their date nights, before the Frenchman took him to bed for hours of passionate lovemaking.

There was no denying the chemistry he and Nico had shared from the moment Nico first walked into the high-end restaurant where Elijah had been based and convinced him to join him at Perrault. They worked together for eight months before Elijah finally gave in to the chef's advances and agreed to go out with him. Though Elijah knew Nico had loved him in his own way during the two years they were together, he had always yearned for more. He was aware from Nico's past relationships, which had been widely advertised in the tabloids, that the French chef had a fear of commitment. And commitment was something Elijah valued highly.

He wasn't the kind of man who was into casual affairs or one-night stands.

The day Elijah walked in on Nico cheating on him with one of their male waiters, he realized that mutual attraction and amazing sex were not enough to sustain their relationship and he had broken things off with the French chef who had become the darling of the Paris gastronomy scene.

The breakup ended up being providential as it gave Elijah the perfect excuse to move back home for a fresh start and to accomplish the dream he'd yearned after for years, which was to open the small town bakery he and his grandmother had once talked about.

Elijah looked surreptitiously at Carter as the latter drank his wine.

That fact that Carter appeared to have the same fear of commitment as Nico from what he'd read about him should have made Elijah nervous. Except he knew Carter had been sincere when he said he wanted to give their relationship a serious try.

Besides, there was one thing Elijah could not deny.

He was wildly attracted to Carter, so much so he got butterflies just being in the same room as the actor. And the intimate kisses and acts they had shared on Carter's porch a few nights past would go down in Elijah's memories as one of the most wickedly sensual things he'd ever done with another man with his clothes still on.

Maisie insisted on both Nico and Elijah reading her a bedtime story. Carter leaned in the bedroom doorway and watched them broodingly, his irritation rolling off him in thick waves. He tucked Maisie in after she fell asleep and followed Elijah and Nico down the stairs.

The two men had just walked out of the house

when Carter snatched Elijah's hand, hauled him back inside the foyer, and closed the door on the stunned Frenchman's face.

"*What the—*" Nico hissed loudly from outside. "Hey, you two had better not get up to any hanky panky in there!"

Nico's protests faded as blood filled Elijah's ears in a dull roar. Carter had crowded him against the door and was taking his mouth in a hungry, possessive kiss.

Elijah responded eagerly, desire sending a shiver shooting through him.

Their heated breaths mingled as they kissed and sucked on each other's lips and tongues, Elijah's cock stiffening painfully behind the zipper of his jeans.

Carter slid his hands down Elijah's back and took a firm hold of his ass.

"You have no idea how badly I want to put my panky inside your hanky right now," he mumbled against Elijah's lips, grinding their erections together.

Elijah gasped and clenched his fingers on Carter's shoulders at the delicious sensation of their rubbing cocks.

"Me too. I want you." Elijah closed his teeth on Carter's lower lip and bit him gently before licking the soft wound. "Inside me. Above me. Under me as I ride you."

Carter's hips jacked forward at Elijah's hot words. "Jesus, you're killing me," he groaned, dropping his forehead against Elijah's.

A muffled pounding startled them. They'd forgotten all about Nico.

"Are you two still there?!"

Elijah sighed at the French chef's outraged tone. "I'd better go take care of that." He chuckled when Carter's eyes rounded in horror. "I don't mean it that way." He kissed Carter's cheek. "Trust me, the only man I want inside me is you. And I can't wait for that to happen."

Carter reluctantly let go of Elijah when the latter turned and took hold of the door knob. "How long is Nico staying at your place?"

"He's going to L.A. in two days." Elijah hesitated. "And I'm sorry again. About letting him stay over. He's still my friend, despite everything that's happened between us."

Carter sighed and pressed a soft kiss to Elijah's lips. "You're too generous for your own good. Then again, that's one of the many things I like about you." His voice grew strained. "And two days is too long. I don't think my patience can stretch that long."

Elijah forced himself to step out of the house, Carter's words making his heart pound erratically. He couldn't wait either. He met Nico's hooded gaze with a defiant expression and led the way down the porch steps, conscious of Carter's heated stare on his back.

CHAPTER FIFTEEN

Carter was still thinking about Elijah when he stepped out of his bathroom an hour later. Knowing that he could be having sex with the alluring pastry chef in two days had made him so hard he'd had to give himself a handjob after the two men had left. His phone buzzed just as he sat down on his bed, more relaxed than he'd felt all day.

It was a message from his agent scheduling a call for the next morning.

Carter frowned. There was nothing imminent on his agenda as far as he knew. He texted back a quick reply and had just put his phone down on the nightstand when it buzzed again. He snatched it up irritably and froze when he saw the words on the screen.

Elijah: I'm outside your front door.

Carter shot off the bed. He checked in on Maisie before hurrying down the stairs. The woody scent of Elijah's shampoo tickled his nose when he yanked the front door open. The pastry chef had showered and changed into dark blue pajama bottoms and a white T-shirt.

"Is everything okay?" Carter said anxiously, peering over his shoulder. Bar the porch light, Elijah's place was dark.

Elijah nodded. "Yeah, everything's fine." He paused, his ears reddening. "I just wanted to see you."

Elijah's confession had Carter cursing and pulling him inside the house. He locked the door, took hold of Elijah's face, and kissed him hard. Elijah melted against him, the hitch of his breath a sweet sound Carter would never tire of hearing.

Carter backed Elijah down the hall and into the sitting room, his heart racing. He sat down heavily on a couch, flicked the lamp on the side table on, and pulled Elijah on top of him. Air whooshed out of Elijah when he found himself straddling Carter's lap.

"Is Nico sleeping?" Carter leaned forward and nibbled on Elijah's throat while he ran his hands greedily up and down Elijah's body.

Elijah arched into his touch and breathed out a sigh, head dropping back to give Carter better access. "Yeah. He's out like a light. And Maisie?"

"She's fast asleep." Carter licked and sucked the pulse drumming wildly at the base of Elijah's neck before biting down. He smiled savagely when Elijah gasped and bucked in his hold, his erection brushing against Carter's stomach.

Carter pushed his sweatpants past his hips before pulling Elijah's pajama bottoms down his thighs. A groan left Carter when he exposed Elijah's lusciously aroused cock, the golden light highlighting the rosy color of his shaft and the precum already coating the swollen, glistening head.

Though Carter had performed oral sex on some of the men he'd had sexual encounters with at the exclusive L.A. club where he'd gone seeking male partners, he very much preferred being on the receiving end of blow jobs.

Not so with Elijah. He couldn't wait to get the pastry chef's cock in his mouth and see if he tasted as delectable as he looked.

I want to suck him for hours!

"Carter," Elijah pleaded softly. He rocked his hips against Carter's, his brown eyes glazed with passion.

Carter closed a hand on their throbbing shafts and started rubbing their aching flesh. Elijah's breathing accelerated as he gazed into Carter's eyes, his pupils dilating with pleasure. He gripped Carter's shoulders and started bumping and grinding on Carter's lap, his dick sliding deliciously against Carter's.

Their pants and groans filled the room as Carter stroked them closer and closer to an explosive climax.

Carter suddenly let go of their cocks. "Take over," he ordered Elijah raspily.

Confusion flashed across Elijah's face. He shuddered when Carter ran his hands up his thighs and around his hips to his ass.

Elijah grasped their cocks in one hand and took over the handjob, the color in his cheekbones and the way he looked imploringly into Carter's eyes telling

Carter he very much wanted whatever Carter intended to do next.

Carter ran his fingers all over Elijah's ass, caressing and squeezing the firm, toned globes.

"Can I touch you, Elijah?" he murmured against Elijah's throat. He slipped his fingers in Elijah's crack and slowly spread his buttcheeks open while he kissed his racing pulse.

"Oh God!" Elijah whimpered, shuddering deliciously in Carter's hold. "*Yes!*"

A muffled cry left Elijah when Carter stroked a finger down his cleft to his hot pucker. Carter cursed as Elijah's entrance twitched and spasmed against the pad of his digit.

Carter took a ragged breath and counted slowly to ten, so close to coming he had to bite down hard on his lip. Just the feel of Elijah's sinful heat made him want to explode. He started exploring Elijah's hole, rubbing and teasing the sensitive folds until they softened.

The sexiest sound Carter had ever heard left Elijah when he finally slipped a finger inside Elijah's hungry opening. Carter knew it would have echoed around the room had Elijah not been trying desperately hard to keep his voice down.

Carter cursed as Elijah clamped down on his invading digit. "*Fuck!* You're so tight!" He pulled out and thrust back in slowly, his wet finger dipping slickly through Elijah's convulsing entrance.

Sweat pearled Elijah's upper lip as he writhed on Carter's lap, one hand rubbing their wet cocks briskly while he clutched Carter's shoulder with the other, his breaths shuddering out of his lungs.

Carter waited until he felt Elijah loosen before slipping a second digit inside his throbbing passage, stretching him open while he continued thrusting in and out. Elijah groaned at the invasion and squeezed Carter's fingers.

They both cursed at the wicked sensation.

"*Carter! Carter!*" Elijah chanted softly over and over again as he finally gave it to his urges, his hips rising and falling on Carter's fingers.

Carter pressed hot kisses to Elijah's throat as he fucked Elijah's hole while Elijah stroked their increasingly wet cocks.

"*Oh!*" Elijah suddenly gasped and stiffened above Carter. He dropped his head against Carter's shoulder and bit his flesh as he came, his harsh cries of pleasure muffled by Carter's T-shirt.

Carter's relished the savage love bite, his own orgasm racing up his thighs and down his spine as he carried on plunging his fingers in and out of Elijah's twitching hole, Elijah's hot cum coating his throbbing cock in spurts of thick, musky stickiness.

"Carter," Elijah breathed, shivers of ecstasy quaking through his very core.

Elijah's hot breath against his neck and the way he clenched spasmodically around Carter's fingers finally tipped Carter over the edge. He came violently, his hips jacking off the couch and lifting Elijah with him, his hands clenching on the tight globes of Elijah's ass,

Elijah's name a prayer and a plea tumbling repeatedly from his lips.

CHAPTER SIXTEEN

"WHAT?" CARTER FROZE IN THE ACT OF BUTTERING Maisie's toast. He stared at his cell where it sat on speaker mode on the kitchen counter. "Can you repeat what you just said?"

"Mira has just signed on as an executive producer on your upcoming movie project," his agent said stiffly.

Alarm filled Carter. It was followed by a surge of anger.

"Give me a minute," he said curtly. He arranged Maisie's breakfast on a plate and gave it to the little girl where she sat coloring at the island.

"Thank you, Uncle Carter," Maisie mumbled, tongue stuck out of the corner of her mouth as she concentrated.

"You're welcome, sweetie." Carter dropped a kiss on the little girl's head, grabbed his cup of coffee, and headed out on the back porch with his cell. He closed the door behind him before strolling over to lean on the railing. "You know about my past with Mira, Barbara."

His agent sighed at the other end of the line. "Yeah, I do. You're not the only client of mine who's had the misfortune of stepping on her radar."

Carter frowned. "So you know I would never have agreed to this project had I known she'd be involved, right?"

"I've already spoken to the studio, Carter."

Carter stilled. "And?"

"They're adamant that they will hold you in breach of contract if you refuse to work with Mira."

Carter swore. "Those bastards. They must know how awkward things will get on set if Mira and I come face to face!"

"I hear you, kid," his agent muttered. "And I'm afraid I have more bad news."

Carter scowled. "What could be worse than what you've already told me?"

"Mira wants to meet you. She insisted I pass the message on."

Carter startled. "What? Why?!"

"She didn't say."

Carter hesitated before fisting his hand around his cell. "Tell Mira I'm busy with a personal matter and I can't see her until filming starts."

A strange foreboding dawned inside him as he ended the call.

Mira Peters was one of the most powerful producers in Hollywood. She was also his former lover and the reason why his career had almost ended before it started.

Carter met Mira shortly after he landed his first major movie role. She was older than him by several years and had taken control of their affair from the get go. As a newcomer in the industry, Carter had been content to play the role of the submissive young gigolo. When it became clear that Mira intended to keep him on a short leash, Carter had taken matters into his own hands and ended their liaison.

Their break up had been an ugly spectacle the tabloids had poured over for weeks, mostly because of the lies Mira spun about Carter cheating on her with younger women. It was those stories that had started Carter's loathsome relationship with the paparazzi who would go on to portray him as Hollywood's quintessential bad boy for the next decade.

Although the experience had left a bitter taste in his mouth, Carter had to concede that he'd learned a lot about the movie business through Mira and her entourage. Had it not been for those contacts and his inherent talents, Carter's career would have fizzled out there and then. At the end of his three-month affair with Mira, Carter had promised himself that he would never get involved with anyone he was actively working with.

Well, it looks like I'm gonna be stuck with her for the next four months.

Carter's only hope was that his former lover would behave professionally and not let their past interfere with their current venture. That she wanted to see him before the scheduled meetup on the first day of filming at the end of the month made him doubt his wish would actually come true.

He frowned. *She's going to be trouble all right.*

Carter did his best to forget about Mira for the rest of that day. He took Maisie to see her therapist and drove into town at lunchtime to visit Elijah. To Carter's ire, they found an uninvited guest in the bakery's kitchen.

"Nico!" Maisie ran up to the French chef and rose on her tiptoes to peer at what he was making.

"Bonjour, chérie." Nico flashed a winsome smile at the little girl and helped her up on a stool. "Would you like to try one?"

Maisie nodded vigorously, her eyes sparkling as she stared at the glazed pastries.

"It's a special serving of savory dishes," Elijah said apologetically to Carter while the Frenchman plated up a tart. "He insisted on making some for my customers."

"Is that his new plan of attack?" Carter grumbled. "Trying to win you over with his cooking skills?"

Elijah sighed. "You have to admit that his beef bourguignon is out of this world."

"Yummy!" Golden flakes coated Maisie's lips as she munched happily. "You have to try one, Uncle Carter!"

Despite his misgivings, Carter had to concede that Nico's savory tart did indeed taste as heavenly as his beef bourguignon.

Elijah made pancakes with Maisie during his break while Nico looked on with a tolerant half-smile and Carter sulked in a corner. From the way Elijah's lips kept twitching every time he glanced at Carter, Carter's increasingly grumpy mood was only serving to amuse him.

Elijah's ears reddened when Carter started staring broodingly at his mouth. He flashed Carter an exasperated *Stop that!* look that had Carter grinning for the first time that day and recalling just how hot Elijah had looked in his arms last night as Carter brought him to an earth-shattering climax.

"He is good with children, *non?*" Nico murmured.

Carter looked at the French chef. Surprise darted through him.

Nico's face was strangely wistful as he gazed at Elijah and Maisie.

"Do you want kids?" Carter said. He regretted the words as soon as they left his mouth.

Nico did not look in the least bit insulted by the brazen question. "Maybe." His mouth twisted in a grimace. "After all, it is in our genes to want to procreate." He paused. "I had hoped it might be with him, one day."

Carter studied Elijah. There was no denying that he was amazing with Maisie. He was aware this had as much to do with Elijah's charming personality as it did with his pure, kind heart.

"You look at him the same way that I do," Nico said suddenly.

Carter met the Frenchman's shrewd eyes guardedly. "And how is that?"

Nico's expression sobered as he stared at Elijah.

"Like you want to cherish him. Because he is the most precious thing to you."

Carter's heart thudded against his ribs as the Frenchman's words rang in his ears. He recalled what he'd said to Nico yesterday, when he'd walked in on his rival kissing Elijah. That he was falling in love for the first time in his life.

The butterflies in his stomach. The way his chest tightened whenever he was around Elijah. His raging desire to take Elijah and make him his.

That was when Carter realized the shocking truth.

He was already in love with Elijah.

"I haven't given up, you know." Nico narrowed his eyes at Carter, as if he'd read his mind. "I want Elijah to come back to Paris with me. I am serious, Carter."

Carter studied the Frenchman steadily. "So am I."

ELIJAH TOWELED HIS HAIR BRISKLY AS HE STEPPED OUT OF the bathroom later that night.

Nico was sitting on his bed with a determined expression.

"Come to L.A. with me tomorrow."

Elijah frowned at his former lover before heading over to the dresser. "Not happening." He grabbed a T-shirt and had just shrugged it over his head and his pajama bottoms, when he felt Nico step up behind him.

"Elijah."

Elijah stiffened as Nico ran his hands lightly down the sides of his ribcage to his waist and hips. It was a classic Nico move meant to seduce him. The Frenchman turned him around slowly.

"I've missed you, *chéri*," Nico murmured, his eyes darkening with desire. He took hold of Elijah's chin and leaned in.

Elijah pressed his fingers to Nico's lips. "No," he said sternly.

Irritation clouded Nico's face. He grabbed Elijah's wrist, pinned his arms behind his back, and crowded him against the chest of drawers before taking his mouth in a forceful kiss full of passion.

Elijah scowled when Nico's erection pressed against him.

This asshole is really pushing his limits tonight!

He raised his right heel and stamped heavily on Nico's left foot.

"Ouch!" Nico let go of Elijah and pulled back, his expression hurt. "That was uncalled for."

"Really?" Elijah jabbed a finger angrily in Nico's chest. "That's my line, Nico. I've told you a dozen times. We are over. And I don't appreciate being kissed against my will!"

A muscle worked in Nico's jawline as he stared at Elijah. "What will it take?"

Elijah blinked. "Excuse me?"

"What will it take to make you fall back in love with me?" Nico said, his voice growing tortured.

Elijah gazed blindly at his former lover.

Damnit. He really is deadly serious about this, isn't he?

Nico narrowed his eyes. "Is it him?"

"What?" Elijah mumbled.

"Is it Carter?" Nico's hands fisted at his sides. "Are you in love with him?"

Heat flooded Elijah's face. "I—" He faltered, shocked by the emotion swirling through him.

Was he already in love with Carter?

Nico scowled. "I *will* make you mine again."

CHAPTER SEVENTEEN

Carter stepped inside the restaurant's foyer and removed his sunglasses. The hostess's eyes widened when she saw him. She signaled to the maître hotêl, who wandered over hastily.

"Mr. Wilson, we were not expecting you," the man gushed in a warm voice, coming forward to shake Carter's hand. "I'm sure we can find you a table."

"It's all right," Carter said in clipped tones. "I'm meeting someone."

Carter had a few seconds to observe the woman he'd come to see while the maître hotêl led him through the busy restaurant. He ignored the murmurs and stares of the other diners and focused on his former lover, the fury twisting his gut masked behind a composed expression.

Mira Peters sat with her back straight, her gaze on the sunny boulevard outside the popular, high-end Italian place she'd picked for their meeting. Her short black hair was impeccably styled in a bob and her white Prada suit fitted her slender body perfectly.

The only sign that she was nervous was the way her crimson-tipped fingers played slightly with the stem of a glass of what Carter knew would be her favorite wine.

Mira looked around when Carter stopped at the table. She watched impassively while he took his seat and ordered a salad and water.

"You're not drinking?" She arched a sculpted eyebrow.

"I'm driving straight back home after this." Carter crossed an ankle across his knee and leaned back in his seat, hoping he appeared as relaxed as he was aiming for. "Why did you want to see me, Mira? I'm busy and I don't appreciate you pressuring Barbara into forcing me to come here today."

A faint smile curved Mira's lips. "Why, have you got a new lover you'd rather be spending your time with?"

Carter narrowed his eyes, Elijah's face floating briefly before his face. "I can't see how that's any of your business."

Mira took a sip of her drink. "Oh, I can make it my business, Carter."

Carter gritted his teeth at her mildly threatening tone. *Here we go.*

"Last I checked, my contract with the studio didn't dictate who I could and couldn't fuck," he said coldly.

A couple of diners looked over, their eyes rounding slightly as they caught his words. Mira's expression grew displeased.

"I have another appointment in two hours," Carter continued briskly. "As you are well aware, I am now the guardian to a little girl who desperately needs my attention. Just say what you've got to say and I'll be on my way. I don't want to see you unless it concerns our upcoming project."

Mira twirled her glass slightly, seemingly unaffected by his curt tone. "Her name is Maisie, isn't it?"

For some reason, the sound of his niece's name on his ex-lover's lips sent a chill down Carter's spine. A waiter came over with their food, the maître hotêl hovering closely to make sure they were happy with their meals. Carter thanked the men and took a bite of his salad after they left.

It was clear from Mira's behavior that whatever she wanted to talk about had nothing to do with the movie they were contracted to work on.

She's up to something.

Mira tucked into her meal, her serene face putting Carter on edge.

Carter had just taken another mouthful of his food when she spoke again.

"I met someone very interesting the other day."

Carter remained silent, his senses on high alert while he chewed and swallowed.

"He's a newbie. You know, one of those young actors who just *loves* to please people."

Carter stabbed at his salad, knowing full well she was taking a dig at him. He'd been like that too when he first came to Hollywood.

Don't let her bait you.

"So what? Is this guy your new protégé?" he snapped.

"No, he isn't." Mira smiled. "He's gay."

Ice filled Carter's veins at the movie producer's words. He had a sudden premonition where this conversation was heading.

"He was telling me a story about this man he couldn't get out of his mind," Mira continued. "A guy he met at one of those upscale private clubs where no one knows each other's identity? He's a friend of the owner, otherwise he wouldn't have gotten in." She paused. "Apparently, the mystery man who rocked his world that night had a birthmark in a really intimate place."

A low buzzing sounded in Carter's ears. He forced himself to take another bite of his food. It tasted like ash in his mouth.

Carter met Mira's hard stare with an inscrutable expression as he went through a quick mental checklist of the men he'd slept with in the last few months. He barely spoke to the guys he had sex with at the club and had never exchanged contact details with any of them. There was no way of knowing if one of them had been an aspiring actor.

"Why are you telling me this, Mira?" He raised his glass of water to his lips and took a low sip, surprised his hand was so steady.

Mira sat back in her chair, her smile widening. "Because I'm wondering if that guy was you, Carter.

Not many men in this town have a heart-shaped birthmark behind their right testicle."

Carter's heart thumped violently.

"Imagine if the tabloids found out that Hollywood's biggest bad boy might actually like dick more than pussy," Mira added in a saccharine tone. "That would be bad for your career."

Carter clenched his jaw. *I can't believe this bitch!*

"You have thirty minutes to get to the point, Mira. Don't waste it with irrelevant stories."

Lines furrowed Mira's brow at Carter's glacial voice.

"I want you back."

Shock jolted Carter. He blinked. "I'm sorry, what?"

"It was wrong of me to break things up with you the way I did." Mira reached across the table and ran her fingers lightly across the back of Carter's hand, her scarlet nails stark against his tanned skin. "I want you back in my life. As my lover."

Carter's flesh crawled at her touch. He resisted the urge to withdraw his hand, his knuckles whitening on his fork. "Is that why you took on this project? To get back in my pants?!"

The couple at the next table looked over again at his angry hiss. Mira's eyes grew cool.

"Don't be crass, Carter." She pulled back and folded her hands primly on her lap. "I miss you. The lovers I've had since we broke up pale in comparison with what we had. You truly were the best at satisfying me in bed."

Carter's pulse raced as he stared at Mira. He barely recognized the woman before him.

She's crazy!

Carter couldn't believe Mira would go to such lengths to sleep with him. He would have been flattered if he'd sensed she genuinely cared for him. Except he knew she didn't.

For Mira, this was about control. He'd inadvertently landed back in her line of sight and she wanted to play her sick power games with him again.

Carter wiped his mouth with his napkin, took a hundred-dollar bill from his wallet, and threw it on the table as he rose to his feet.

"Newsflash, lady. *I* dumped *you*. And there is no way I would ever have you back. So you can take your thinly veiled remarks and go to hell, Mira."

CHAPTER EIGHTEEN

Nervous anticipation bubbled inside Elijah as he stepped onto Carter's porch. He knocked on the door, the bottle of wine in his right hand cool against his skin. To his surprise, it was Maisie who opened the door.

"Hi, sweetie."

Maisie's eyes widened. "Elijah!" She grabbed his hand and pulled him inside the house. "Come help, quick!"

Elijah chuckled. "What's wrong?" He stiffened when an acrid smell teased his nostrils. "Wait. Is something burning?!"

Carter was cursing liberally when Maisie and Elijah rushed inside the kitchen. He waved at the smoke curling up from the pots in front of him before switching the vent fan on and opening the back door.

"Uncle Carter is saying naughty words," Maisie mumbled to Elijah.

Carter jumped slightly and whirled around, finally noticing their presence.

Elijah studied his preoccupied expression with a faint frown. "Is everything okay?"

Carter hesitated before nodding. "Yeah. I was making dinner and got distracted." He looked mournfully at his niece. "I'm sorry about the bad words."

Elijah wandered over to the range and stared into the charred casserole dishes while Carter dropped a kiss on Maisie's head and picked her up in his arms.

"What were you trying to make?"

Carter grimaced. "You'll laugh if I tell you."

Elijah's gaze landed on an open cookbook on the counter. His eyes widened when he read the title of the recipe. He bit his lip. "You were trying to cook beef bourguignon?"

Carter sighed. "You're laughing."

"I'm not," Elijah said in a strangled voice, shoulders shaking.

They ended up ordering pizza and ate it straight out of the box, much to Maisie's delight.

"I'm sorry you went to the trouble of getting that expensive bottle of wine," Carter mumbled after they'd put the little girl to bed later that night.

"We can drink it another time."

They were sitting in Carter's kitchen, enjoying a cup of coffee.

"And I'm sorry," Carter added. "About tonight."

Elijah startled guiltily.

"We were meant to, you know—" Carter paused, an awkward look on his face.

Elijah flushed. "I—it's okay! I can—" He stopped, mortified.

Carter stared before bursting out laughing. "Were you about to say that you can wait to have sex with me? 'Cause if you were, I feel I should be deeply offended."

"Now who's laughing at whom?" Elijah grumbled, his ears hot.

A companionable silence filled the kitchen as they finished their drinks.

"Did something happen?" Elijah finally murmured, putting down his empty cup. "You're not acting like your normal self."

Carter's expression grew guarded. He climbed off the breakfast stool and took their cups over to the sink.

Tension coiled through Elijah as he observed Carter's stiff back. He'd never seen the actor like this. "Carter?"

Carter seemed to reach some sort of decision. He twisted on his heels and strode over to Elijah, his expression determined. Surprise jolted Elijah when Carter took his hands.

"I have something to tell you. It's a story from my past." Carter paused, a strangely vulnerable look darkening his hazel eyes. "Will you listen to it?"

Elijah dipped his chin, now more than a little anxious.

Carter started to talk. As he described his encounter with the movie producer he'd met on his first major film project and relayed the details of their subsequent affair, Elijah's anxiety turned to dread.

"Mira was like no woman I had ever met before." A muscle jumped in Carter's cheek. "I was bedazzled by her beauty and her success, and I was more than a little grateful for her attention. It took a while for me to realize that she was taking control of my life. Once I did, I broke things off." He ran distracted fingers through his hair before taking hold of Elijah's hands again. "It was messy. And it was the first time I started appearing in all the tabloids. Mira pulled no punches in the tales she spun to the media and accused me of cheating on her with several younger women."

"She sounds like a real piece of work," Elijah murmured.

Carter grimaced. "You have no idea."

Elijah hesitated before asking the question that was troubling him the most.

"Did you love her?"

"No." Carter shook his head. "We had great chemistry in bed and I enjoyed her company, but I never fell in love with her."

Elijah's heart pounded in his chest as he gazed at Carter. "Then, why are you telling me this? Are you—" he paused and swallowed, "are you thinking of getting back together with her?"

Horror widened Carter's eyes. "Hell no!" he said vehemently, his grip tightening on Elijah's fingers. "I can't stand Mira! The reason I'm telling you about her is because she just signed on as a producer on my next movie and forced me into having a meeting with her this morning. She suspects I'm gay and she threatened to go public if I didn't agree to enter into another relationship with her."

Elijah almost fell off his chair in shock. "What? Is she insane?!"

"Exactly." Carter scowled. "I've already spoken to my agent. I want to be ready if Mira goes to the press with this story."

Dismay filled Elijah then. He looked down at their entwined fingers, troubled by the thought that had been at the back of his mind since he first read up on Carter.

"Is that why I never saw anything in the media about you being bi? You didn't want people to find out about your sexuality?"

Tense silence fell between them.

Carter sighed before tilting Elijah's chin up gently with a knuckle. "I've kept this a secret pretty much all of my adult life because I was afraid of the possible repercussions on my career. I've seen what happens when Hollywood turns its back on someone because of their sexual preferences. I had too much at stake for that to happen."

Pain twisted Elijah's chest at Carter's words. He took a shaky breath. "I don't want to be a dirty little secret, Carter. I am proud of who I am, gay and all. I have no intention of hiding my sexuality if we become a couple."

Carter leaned his forehead against Elijah's. "I know," he said softly. "Which is why I spoke to my lawyers this afternoon."

Elijah stared at him, puzzled.

"We're preparing a public relations damage limitation statement for when I come out of the closet."

Elijah's heart stuttered. "You said when," he blurted after a shocked pause. "Not if, but when."

Carter pressed a soft kiss to Elijah's lips. "I very much want this relationship, Elijah." He stared into Elijah's eyes as he rubbed their noses together. "You may end up having to look after Maisie and me if I can't land another movie role when this story breaks."

Emotion nearly choked Elijah at Carter's teasing tone. He couldn't believe the actor was willing to take such a huge risk for him. He raised trembling hands to Carter's face. "I may not be able to keep you in the lavish lifestyle you're accustomed to, but I can definitely support you and Maisie."

Carter smiled at his fervent tone. "I'm counting on it."

CHAPTER NINETEEN

"Got any plans for the rest of the weekend?" Sam said as they locked up on Saturday evening.

Elijah shook his head. "I think it'll be a quiet one. Carter said he was busy with something."

"I love how you automatically mentioned Carter there," Sam said drily. "How are things going? Is the dark-haired bombshell from Paris still cockblocking you guys?"

Elijah sighed. "No, Nico's still in L.A."

"So, have you and Carter done, you know—" Sam waggled her eyebrows and made suggestive movements with her fingers, "the wicked deed yet?"

Elijah flushed at Sam's grin. "No comment."

Sam laughed before climbing on her moped and speeding away.

Elijah got home a while later and glanced across the road. Carter's home was dark. Disappointment flitted through him.

Looks like I won't be seeing him tonight either.

It had been six days since Carter had told him about Mira and what had transpired at their meeting in L.A. With Maisie coming along in leaps and bounds, her therapist had advised Carter enroll her in a preschool club for the summer. Carter had gone to L.A. to check out places close to his Malibu home and the studio. With his movie project on the horizon, the actor was going to be busier than ever with his career and the little girl who had become the focus of his life.

Elijah squashed the selfish feelings that had been festering inside him all week and went inside his house. He put the TV on, poured himself a glass of wine, and had just settled on the couch when the doorbell chimed. He rose to his feet and strolled over to check the peephole.

Carter was standing on his porch in a stylish black suit and red tie.

Elijah's heart soared. He undid the latch and opened the door, trying hard not to show just how pleased he was. "Hey." He looked past Carter's shoulder. The house opposite was still dark. "Where's Maisie?" Elijah said, puzzled.

"Izzy and Wyatt have her for the weekend." Carter's eyes sparkled as he gazed at Elijah. "How about you get dressed and join me?"

Elijah stared at Carter's elegant attire. "What's going on?"

A sexy smile curved Carter's mouth. "I'm wining and dining you tonight." He took Elijah's left hand and lifted it to his mouth before pressing a kiss to his knuckles, his lips practically scorching Elijah's skin. "And I'm really looking forward to dessert."

Understanding dawned inside Elijah. Heat flooded his cheeks.

"Give me fifteen minutes," he mumbled, his heart now thumping hard.

Carter was waiting for him on the porch when Elijah stepped out of the house a short while later.

"You scrub up nice." Carter took in Elijah's chic blue suit, cream shirt, and gold tie with an admiringly stare. He came up to Elijah, stroked his knuckles gently across Elijah's left cheek, and leaned in to whisper in his ear. "But I gotta say, I *really* love your white chef uniform. I've been dreaming about peeling that off your body ever since I first saw you in it."

Oh God.

Elijah almost melted into a puddle of lust as Carter's husky voice reverberated through his very body. It was bad enough that he'd spent the time he'd showered and gotten ready fantasizing about Carter making love to him tonight. Now that the man had turned the charm factor up by a hundred percent, Elijah feared he wouldn't last past the first course.

Surprise rushed through him when they headed across the road and strolled past Carter's car.

"I thought we were going out."

Carter smiled and led him up the porch of the dark house. "I made dinner."

Elijah had barely gotten over his astonishment

when they stepped inside the foyer. He stilled as the most delicious aroma wafted over him. That was when he saw the candles lighting up a path through the house.

"Oh."

Elijah's pulse accelerated as they followed the trail to the kitchen. He faltered, his eyes widening.

A golden glow filled the room from the candles dotting the space. Elijah's gaze fell on the dining table to the left.

Carter had prepped it with a red cloth and white napkins, fine cream China and crystal glasses, and a dozen pale pink roses in a porcelain vase.

"Wow." Elijah turned to Carter, so happy he couldn't hide his grin. "You sure know how to impress a guy."

Carter looped his arms around Elijah's waist and pressed his lips to his brow. "You're the first man I'm doing this with," he admitted quietly. "And I gotta say, I'm all kinds of nervous."

Elijah blinked. This close, he could feel the tension humming through Carter and the way the actor's heart was pounding in his chest.

"The guys I slept with always wore masks, so we never saw each other's faces. And I never met any of them outside the club," Carter said ruefully. "As for the women I had sex with, it was always at their place or a hotel." His hands tightened on Elijah's back. "You're the first person I'm inviting into my home and my bed, Elijah."

Elijah had to clench his fists hard to stop himself from kissing Carter and dragging him upstairs to the bedroom right then.

"Elijah?" Carter said hesitantly.

"I want to make love with you so bad right now," Elijah murmured against Carter's throat. "But I'm also curious to see what you made for dinner. It smells heavenly."

Carter grinned and dropped a quick peck on his lips. "I had a chef I'm friends with in L.A. show me how to make it." He led Elijah to the table and pulled out a chair. "Why don't you pour us some wine while I bring the food over?"

Elijah smiled when he lifted the bottle sitting in the wine bucket. It was the one he'd brought over last weekend, on the night they'd first planned to have sex.

They had a delectable goat cheese salad for a starter. But it was the main course that had Elijah's stomach rumbling in anticipation.

"Is that Coq au Vin?" He stared at the sumptuous dish Carter had just plated up for him.

"Yup. You have no idea how many of these I ruined before I got it right."

Elijah chuckled as Carter took the seat opposite him. A moan of appreciation left him when he bit into the juicy chicken a moment later. "This is incredible, Carter."

"Coming from a chef of your caliber, I'll take that as a compliment." Carter took a sip of his wine, his gaze growing heated. "By the way, have I told you how much I love watching you eat? It's like everything you put in your mouth tastes divine."

Elijah blushed, his mind bringing up all sorts of fanciful, lewd images.

From the way Carter grinned, it was clear he could tell what was going through Elijah's head.

Dessert was a vanilla and whiskey crème brûlée that Carter had picked up from a famous restaurant in L.A. that afternoon. They headed out to the porch for coffee and sat in companionable silence for a while, the star-lit heavens shining down on them.

"How did it go with Maisie's preschool?" Elijah said.

"I've decided to enroll her in one here, in Twilight Falls."

Elijah stared at Carter.

"Maisie is happy here," Carter explained quietly at Elijah's startled expression. He took Elijah's hand in his own and gazed out at the dark forest. "I've also decided to keep living here for the time being. There'll be times when I'll have to stay in L.A. because of my filming schedule, but I would rather have you and my friends look after Maisie than strangers."

Elijah's fingers clenched spasmodically around Carter's. Once again, the actor had managed to surprise him. "You're pretty amazing, you know that?"

Carter chuckled at his heartfelt tone. "I'm hoping you'll still think that after tonight."

Elijah's breath caught in his throat. Carter's expression sobered. Slow-burning sexual tension filled the space between them. Carter took their cups, pulled Elijah to his feet, and guided him inside the house.

They headed up the stairs to Carter's bedroom, Carter's pulse thumping violently against Elijah's skin where he still had a hold of Elijah's hand. Elijah knew Carter could feel his own heartbeat hammering away at his wrist.

Carter let go of Elijah long enough to draw the curtains and light the candles he'd set around the room.

"Nervous?" He came up to Elijah and stroked his hands down his arms where he stood next to the bed.

"Kinda." Elijah shivered at the heat coiling through his body and sparking between their skin. "I've built this up so much in my head."

Carter took hold of Elijah's chin and brushed his lips across his. "So have I. I can't wait to be inside you."

Elijah's dick throbbed at the desire lighting Carter's eyes.

Carter proceeded to undress Elijah slowly, his fingers lingering on Elijah's sensitized skin as he peeled away layer after layer of clothing. Elijah shuddered when Carter removed his briefs, freeing his erect cock from its tight confines. To Elijah's shock, Carter removed his red silk tie from his collar and wrapped it around Elijah's wrists.

"I really want to make love to you." Carter laid a firm hand on Elijah's chest and pushed him back toward the bed. Elijah gasped when Carter tumbled him backward onto the sheets. "But first, I really, *really* want to blow you."

Carter hooked powerful hands under Elijah's hips

and hauled him to the edge of the mattress so his legs dangled to the floor.

"Hands above your head, Elijah," Carter ordered silkily as he dropped to his knees.

Elijah obeyed the command automatically, so turned on he thought he might pass out. Carter taking charge of their lovemaking was sexy as hell.

CHAPTER TWENTY

Carter settled between Elijah's thighs and ran his hands up and down Elijah's quivering legs, his heart racing.

Elijah's body was as intoxicating as he'd imagined it would be. With his toned, beautifully-defined muscles and honey-colored skin, the pastry chef looked like the finest meal Carter had ever seen as he lay submissively on his bed. Carter licked his lips, intent on savoring Elijah to the very last drop. The way Elijah was responding to him had him so fired up though, he thought he might blow his load any moment.

Elijah gazed hotly at Carter when Carter slowly spread his thighs open. He shuddered as Carter pressed his mouth tenderly to the head of his swollen cock.

"Carter," Elijah moaned.

Carter ran his tongue down Elijah's shaft all the way to the root and back up again, exploring his heated flesh with teasing, sensuous flicks.

Delicious.

Carter got Elijah all nice and wet before wrapping his lips around the tip of his shivering cock and sucking. Elijah cried out, his whole body tensing on the bed.

Carter closed his eyes as he slowly took Elijah's cock deeper inside his mouth, rolling his tongue around his sensitive length to taste him fully.

Shit! I really could suck him for hours!

Carter started blowing Elijah in earnest, hungry for more of his sinful flavor.

"Carter! Carter!"

Carter opened his eyes at Elijah's breathless chant. The sight that met him made him groan and drop a hand to his own throbbing erection.

Elijah was shuddering and writhing on the bed, his bound hands gripping the sheets above his head tightly, his eyes wide and his face flushed with pleasure. His hips rolled in a wickedly seductive dance as he started plunging his dick in and out of Carter's mouth.

Carter held on to Elijah's thighs and bobbed his head up and down in time with Elijah's thrusts, Elijah's precum coating his tongue thickly as he sucked and licked and flicked his shaft.

"Oh God!"

Elijah's tortured cry resonated in Carter's ears when he took him all the way to the back of his throat. He could tell Elijah was close to coming from the way he was shoving his shaft erratically in and out of Carter's mouth, toes flexing where he pressed his feet against the floor and ass rising jerkily off the bed.

Carter slowed down and let go of Elijah's plump

dick with a wet, popping sound that made his own cock pulse and drew a moan of protest from Elijah.

Carter smiled and gently sucked one of Elijah's balls into his mouth.

Elijah grunted, hips jerking and a jet of precum shooting from his aroused cock.

Carter carried on tormenting Elijah, alternating between pressing hot kisses to the inside of Elijah's thighs and his trembling belly, and sucking on his cock and balls.

By the time Elijah exploded at the back of Carter's throat, he was almost sobbing with pleasure and his body was coated in a fine sheen of sweat.

Carter swallowed Elijah's seed greedily, the musky taste and scent causing his own cock to leak precum. He rose, stripped hastily out of his clothes, and wedged a pillow under Elijah's hips, raising his lower body off the bed.

"Carter?" Elijah murmured in a sated voice, his brown eyes dark with pleasure as he blinked them open. He lifted his head off the sheets and tugged his lower lip sexily between his teeth when he spied Carter's impressive arousal.

Carter removed a box of condoms and a bottle of lube from the nightstand drawer and dropped them on the bed. Then he was down on his knees again.

He took hold of Elijah's legs and hooked them over his shoulders.

Elijah's eyes widened. "Carter. You don't have to—"

"I want to." Carter met Elijah's shocked gaze fervently. "I want to taste every inch of you!"

He spread Elijah's thighs open, exposing the tantalizing strip of skin under his balls and his sexy pucker. Carter licked his lips before leaning in and blowing out a gentle breath over Elijah's hole.

Elijah gasped and arched, his heels digging into Carter's shoulder blades.

"*Fuck!* That feels good!"

Carter's heart thumped against his ribs he brought his mouth to Elijah's hole. He had never rimmed a man before. He flicked his tongue lightly against the tight folds guarding Elijah's opening.

He might as well have set off a bomb the way Elijah jerked and cried out.

Carter grew bolder as he started exploring Elijah's sinful entrance with his tongue and lips. He grabbed the lube, poured a generous amount on his fingers, and brought them into play.

❦

Elijah could barely put a coherent thought together as Carter slipped a lube-slicked finger inside him while he continued rimming him with his mouth.

He's driving me crazy!

His body was still buzzing from the incredible orgasm Carter had just given him. Yet, his dick was starting to stir again, the sparks of electricity shooting through him from where Carter was playing with his ass causing blood to rush to his spent flesh.

An intense bolt of pleasure drew a loud cry from Elijah as Carter pushed a second finger inside him and found his prostate. Elijah's cock hardened in an instant. He lifted his head off the mattress and reached down with his bound hands, his fingers finding Carter's hair.

"Carter! I—" Elijah gasped as Carter flexed his fingers and pressed against his prostate again, sending another dizzying jolt of ecstasy through his very core. *"Fuck!"*

Carter lifted his head slightly from where he was eating Elijah's hole and flashed Elijah a dirty smile.

"I believe I *am* fucking you, Mr. Davis."

He thrust inside Elijah over and over again, his fingers massaging and kneading his sweet spot. Elijah groaned, his cock pulsing out precum with every wicked jab.

He shuddered when Carter reached up and wrapped a lube-slicked hand around his straining shaft. Then he lost himself to the most insane pleasure as Carter stroked his cock, fucked him with his fingers, and rimmed his hole with his tongue.

A buzzing started in Elijah's head as his orgasm built in intense waves deep inside his belly, causing all his muscles to tense and his ass to clench, his entrance squeezing Carter tighter and tighter.

Elijah's tortured shout reached his own ears dimly as he came with stunning violence, his vision throbbing with white flashes of light, his fingers clutching Carter's hair in a punishing grip, jet after jet of hot cum splashing all the way up his body to his chest and neck.

CHAPTER TWENTY-ONE

CARTER'S BLOOD THRUMMED SAVAGELY IN HIS VEINS AS he slowly withdrew his fingers from Elijah's body and climbed to his feet, his erection throbbing painfully where it stood at full mast between his thighs. Elijah panted and trembled where he lay on Carter's bed, his limbs and belly quivering with powerful aftershocks of pleasure, his face and chest glistening with sweat.

Carter had never seen anything as erotic as Elijah in the midst of a climax. And he couldn't wait to make Elijah come all over again, this time with his cock wedged deep inside his sweet hole.

Elijah's eyes fluttered open when Carter slipped the pillow out from under him and climbed on the bed. Carter maneuvered Elijah farther up the sheets and settled his body slowly on top of his.

Elijah shivered when Carter's erection pressed into his belly. "Wow. That's quite a hard on."

Carter smiled and worked his fingers in Elijah's

damp hair before taking his lips in a long, deep kiss. He rolled his body sensuously up and down Elijah's.

Elijah clutched Carter's shoulders and arched up into him, his legs dropping open to accommodate Carter in the cradle of his thighs.

"You realize where your mouth has just been, right?" Elijah mumbled against Carter's lips when he ended their torrid kiss.

Carter grinned. "Your dessert was incredibly tasty." He rubbed his nose against Elijah's. "I very much want to eat it again."

The way Elijah flushed at his filthy words made Carter chuckle. His laughter turned into a groan when Elijah reached down between their bodies and stroked Carter's swollen cock.

"Not fair. You've made me come twice and you haven't come even once yet." Elijah nipped at Carter's jawline with his teeth, passion darkening his eyes once more. "Want me to blow you?"

"I do," Carter admitted in a rough voice. "But first, I want to make love to you."

Carter kissed Elijah again before moving his mouth to Elijah's ears and throat. Elijah melted against him as he started exploring his body with his lips, tongue, and hands. Carter sucked Elijah's nipples until his nubs were stiff and red before raining kisses down his trembling six-pack. He nipped playfully at Elijah's belly with his teeth and smiled when Elijah grabbed his head and shuddered, the love bites causing his swollen cock to twitch wetly against Carter's chest.

Carter reached for the box of condoms, ripped one

open with his teeth, and sheathed himself under Elijah's heated gaze. He coated his trembling erection liberally with lube and rolled Elijah onto his front.

Carter slipped a pillow under Elijah's belly before settling his body against Elijah's. They both shuddered at the intimate contact, Carter's cock coming to rest enticingly against Elijah's crack. Carter caressed and kissed Elijah's nape and back, exploring every inch of him like he'd told him he would, his heart thundering wildly in his chest.

Carter couldn't get enough of Elijah. Making love with the person he was losing his heart to was a whole different ballgame to having casual sex with a stranger.

"Carter?" Elijah looked over his shoulder as Carter nibbled on the back of his knees, his chocolate gaze burning with need. "Enter me, please!"

Carter shivered at Elijah's desperate plea. He rose up Elijah's body, gripped Elijah's left hand where Elijah clutched at the bedsheets, and guided his rock-hard erection to Elijah's hole.

Elijah moaned and tilted his ass up as the tip of Carter's cock teased his opening.

Carter pressed home slowly, his gaze on the place where their bodies were merging. Blood thundered in his ears as he watched Elijah's hole spasm before relaxing to accept his dick.

They both panted loudly as Carter pulled on Elijah's butt cheek with a thumb, stretching Elijah's entrance open while he pushed in.

Carter blinked sweat from his eyes and bit his lip hard, so close to coming he could scream. Elijah's fingers clenched on the sheets. A low hiss left his lips as Carter slipped past the tight ring of muscles guarding his passage.

Carter thrust his hips gently. They gasped when he slid fully home, his whole length swallowed by Elijah's tight, intoxicating heat, his pubes teasing Elijah's pucker.

Carter grabbed Elijah's right hand, yanked his arms above his head, pulled his cock halfway out and thrust back inside with a savage sound.

Elijah cried out, his hungry hole tightening around Carter's shaft, his own hips rolling and punching his engorged dick into the bedsheets.

Carter felt his control slipping as he started fucking Elijah, the feel of Elijah's passage so exquisite he was shocked he hadn't climaxed when he entered him. He grunted and tried to slow his powerful thrusts, not wanting to hurt Elijah.

Elijah turned his head, his mouth open on sexy moans and gasps, his pupils dilated with passion. "Harder! *Fuck me harder, Carter!*"

Carter cursed. Then he let loose, his grip punishing as he grasped Elijah's hands and pushed him into the bed, his hips pumping his swollen cock in and out of Elijah's passage. The bed creaked and groaned with the force of their lovemaking, Elijah's sultry cries and Carter's grunts rising above the metallic sounds.

"Carter! Oh God! *Yes!*"

Elijah convulsed violently under Carter as he came, his body writhing and his ass gripping Carter's cock hungrily while his own dick spurted cum all over the bed.

Carter's orgasm raced through his spine and tightened his belly. He arched above Elijah, the most insane waves of ecstasy he'd ever known filling his vision with a red haze and wrenching a hoarse shout from his throat as he finally climaxed. His dick pulsed savagely, filling the condom with his cum as he continued plunging in and out of Elijah.

Carter shuddered and slowed his erratic hips before lowering himself shakily onto Elijah, his body quaking with pleasure while he pressed the man beneath him into the mattress. From the way Elijah trembled and twitched, he was still in the grip of the delicious aftermath of his own orgasm.

"Carter?" Elijah panted a moment later.

"Yeah?" Carter nuzzled Elijah's nape and pressed a kiss against his hot skin.

"You're still erect." Elijah sounded more than a little shocked as he squeezed his hole tentatively.

Carter groaned when Elijah's passage milked his swollen shaft. He couldn't believe he was still aroused either. "I was hoping you wouldn't notice."

"That would be kind of hard."

Carter chuckled. Elijah sucked in air when the action caused Carter's cock to move inside him.

"Ready for round two?" Carter nibbled on Elijah's ear before slipping out of his body and discarding the used condom. He sheathed himself with a fresh rubber, rolled Elijah onto his back, and wrapped Elijah's legs around his waist.

"Should I be worried about your stamina?" Elijah said, his face flushed. He licked his lips when Carter aligned his cock with his entrance.

Carter grinned and slid home in a single smooth thrust. Elijah gasped and closed his eyes at the deep penetration, his head dropping back languidly. Carter closed his left hand on Elijah's hip and wrapped his right hand around Elijah's stirring cock. Elijah shivered when Carter started rubbing him.

"I'm not like this with everyone." Carter leaned down to kiss Elijah's chest and started pumping his hips slowly while he stroked Elijah's growing erection. "Only with you."

Elijah moaned and clutched at Carter's thighs, his hips rising to meet Carter's thrusts, his brown eyes blazing with desire.

CHAPTER TWENTY-TWO

ELIJAH WOKE UP TO A FAINT RINGING. HE OPENED HIS eyes, made to shift his body, and stiffened when he felt something pressing him into the mattress. Elijah looked down just as the ringing stopped.

Carter's head was on his chest, his arms wrapped snuggly around Elijah's waist. His blond hair was tousled and his handsome face relaxed in sleep, his lips parted slightly on slow, deep breaths.

Elijah smiled and stroked a careful finger down Carter's stubbled cheek. It had been a long time since he'd spent an entire night making love and he was pleasantly sore from overexercising muscles he hadn't used in a while. Still, he wouldn't have had it any other way.

Sex with Carter was intoxicating.

Elijah's face warmed when he recalled how Carter had brought him to one earth-shattering climax after another as he toyed with his body, taking his time to learn all of Elijah's pleasure spots. Elijah had returned the favor when he'd sucked and deep-throated Carter to several orgasms that had him cursing out loud in pleasure.

The ringing started again. Elijah raised his head off the pillow. Carter's pants were vibrating on the floor next to the bed.

Carter stirred, eyes fluttering open lazily. He hugged Elijah's body and yawned before looking up. "'Morning." He propped his chin on Elijah's chest, his five-o'clock shadow prickling Elijah's sensitive skin, and flashed a devastating smile at him.

Elijah's heart throbbed. "That should be illegal," he mumbled.

Carter arched an eyebrow. "What should be illegal?" He slipped a hand down Elijah's thigh and caressed his flesh teasingly.

Elijah shuddered, desire pooling in his veins anew.

The sound of the ringing cell finally drew Carter's attention. He slid to the edge of the bed, grabbed the phone from his pants' pocket, and glanced at the screen. He stiffened in the next instant.

"Carter?" Elijah said hesitantly.

Carter scrambled upright and hit the answer button. "Izzy?"

Elijah's stomach dropped when the color drained from Carter's face. Carter reached for Elijah's hand and gripped his fingers tightly as he turned to look at him, his eyes darkening with alarm.

"We're on our way."

❧

"It's an ear infection."

Relief flooded Carter where he held Maisie on his lap. He pressed a tremulous kiss to his niece's head, the adrenaline that had been surging through his body for the last forty minutes abating slightly.

The man took the auroscope out of the little girl's ear. "Well done, Maisie." He smiled and ruffled her hair. "Why don't we get you some special medicine to make you better, huh?"

Maisie nodded sleepily, her cheeks flushed with fever. "Is the medicine bitter?"

Owen White grinned. "Nope, it's as sweet as you are."

Maisie giggled before sucking her thumb into her mouth and closing her eyes, her head falling against Carter's chest. She was asleep within seconds.

"Thank you so much for seeing her," Carter said gratefully as he cradled her. "I know it's your day off." He looked ruefully around the Pediatrician's kitchen. "We're lucky you live so close to Izzy."

"It's no problem," Owen said with a wave of his hand. "Besides, I owe Wyatt and Izzy a favor or two." His gaze shifted to Elijah, who hovered anxiously next to the chair where Carter sat holding Maisie. "You're that guy, aren't you? The famous Paris chef behind *La Petite Bouche Gourmande*?"

Surprise danced across Elijah's face. He glanced at Carter.

"Yes, I am. How did you know?"

Owen grimaced. "The nurses at the hospital can't stop talking about your cakes *or* you." He turned to

Carter while Elijah flushed. "I'll write Maisie a prescription for antibiotics. She should take them for the next five days. Her fever should settle by tomorrow."

"How much do I owe you?" Carter asked. "My insurance paperwork's at home, but I'm happy to pay you outright, especially since you're seeing us on a Sunday, in your own home."

Owen shook his head. "A friend of Izzy's is a friend of mine," he said, his tone adamant. "Besides, I won't have it be said that I was a callous man to *the* Carter Wilson in his time of need."

They left the pediatrician's house a short time later and walked back to Izzy and Wyatt's house, where Elijah had left his car. Elijah kept Maisie company at Izzy and Wyatt's place while Carter drove into town to get his niece's medications. Izzy and Wyatt insisted they stay for lunch when he got back. Though Carter wanted nothing more than to go home and put Maisie to bed, he reluctantly agreed; he owed the pair that much.

"I can get Wyatt to drop Maisie and me home later if you need to go back," Carter told Elijah hesitantly.

Elijah shook his head. "I can stay. It's not like I had anything planned today any way."

Carter put Maisie down on the couch in Izzy and Wyatt's den. He pulled a light blanket over her shoulders, tucked her favorite teddy bear next to her cheek, and made to rise to his feet. Maisie stirred and opened her eyes.

"You can go back to sleep, sweetheart." Carter leaned down and pressed a kiss to her head.

Maisie blinked sleepily. "Love you, Uncle Carter." She looked blearily past Carter. "Love you, Uncle Elijah."

"Love you too, Maisie," Elijah said softly where he leaned against the doorjamb.

Carter's heart swelled with emotion as he gazed at his niece. He turned and headed for the doorway.

Elijah startled when Carter slipped his right hand through his.

"Thank you for coming with me." Carter dropped his head on Elijah's shoulder, suddenly weary. "That was one of the scariest things I've ever experienced. I would have been an utter mess if you hadn't been with me."

Elijah hesitated before hugging Carter. "I seriously doubt that. You're one of the strongest people I know."

Carter raised his head when he felt the tension humming through Elijah. Even though the pastry chef had been doing his best to hide it, Carter had seen how strained Elijah had looked when they were at Owen's house.

"Are you having regrets?" Carter asked quietly, finally giving voice to his fear. "About last night?"

Elijah's eyes widened. "No! I would never—" He faltered, his gaze darkening. "I would never regret anything that happens between us, Carter. I want you to believe that." A muscle jumped in his jawline. "I just feel guilty that you weren't there for Maisie because you were with me."

Carter frowned. He took hold of Elijah's chin and dropped a firm kiss on his lips. "I never want to hear you say that again." His eyes bored into Elijah's. "To be honest, the same thought went through my mind at one point when you were driving me here. But it was my decision to ask Izzy and Wyatt to babysit Maisie. And there's one thing you need to understand." Carter cradled Elijah's face. "You are as important to me as Maisie is, Elijah. Never forget that."

Elijah swallowed convulsively, color staining his cheeks at Carter's candid words. "I—"

"Whoa. Am I interrupting?"

Carter and Elijah startled. They turned and guiltily eyed the man who'd just stepped in the corridor.

Hunter grinned at them.

Carter narrowed his eyes. "What are you doing here?"

"Izzy invited us for lunch." Hunter looked past Carter's shoulder. "I hear the little munchkin is under the weather."

"It's an ear infection. Izzy's friend Owen gave her antibiotics."

Carter and Elijah joined Hunter, Izzy, and Wyatt in the kitchen. Tristan, Drake, Alex, and Finn soon piled through the front door. Despite Carter's misgivings, lunch was a fun affair, his friends' company lightening his and Elijah's moods. Though the others glanced inquisitively at the pair of them from time to time, Carter was grateful they didn't pry. They were all aware of his bisexuality and knew he had never been in a serious relationship. The fact that Elijah was by his side right now made it clear just how special the chef was to Carter.

Although Maisie had become the focus of his life as of late and was the primary reason he'd moved to Twilight Falls, Carter would forever be grateful for the twisted fate that had brought Elijah into his life.

Because one thing had become crystal clear in the last twenty-four hours.

He was head over heels in love with Elijah.

And Carter was determined to have it all. His movie career. Maisie. And the man who had stolen his heart.

CHAPTER TWENTY-THREE

Elijah parked the Citroën outside Carter's house and eyed the Harley-Davidson across the road.

"I see Nico is back," Carter murmured, his tone turning sour.

"Why don't you settle Maisie in?" Elijah suggested. "I'll go see if he's okay and come over later? Dinner's on me tonight."

Carter nodded, kissed Elijah, and carefully got his sleeping niece out of the back of the car. Elijah waited until Carter had gone inside before heading over to his own house.

Nico was making himself a sandwich in the kitchen. "*Bonne après-midi, mon amour. Tu veux un sandwich au steak?*"

"I already had lunch, thanks." Elijah took a bottle of water out of the refrigerator. "And less of the *mon amour*, please. I ceased being your love a long time ago."

"You're hurting my feelings."

Elijah sighed at Nico's teasing tone.

This guy is too confident for his own good.

"So, how was L.A.?"

"Crowded and noisy," Nico admitted.

Elijah leaned against the counter, twisted the cap open, and swallowed a swig of water. "Did you find what you were looking for?"

Nico shrugged. "Maybe." He plated his sandwich, added a drizzle of homemade dressing to his salad, and took a seat at the kitchen table. "There are a couple of promising venues. I want to show them to you."

Elijah studied Nico steadily. "If this is your attempt to get me into bed, it won't—"

Nico put up a hand. "Contrary to popular belief, I don't just have sex on my mind, Elijah." He paused. "I made my intentions toward you clear when I came to Twilight Falls. And I still want you to come back to Paris with me."

Elijah stiffened at his former lover's words.

He really is serious about that, huh?

"And I made it clear I wasn't going to get back together with you or return to Paris." Elijah's voice hardened. "Twilight Falls. The bakery. They mean the world to me, Nico. It was what my grandmother and I always dreamed of."

Nico frowned and leaned back in his chair. "Is it your dream though, Elijah?" he said quietly. "You always wanted to be a pastry chef. Paris is the center of the patisserie world. Your talents will go to waste here."

Elijah's fingers tightened on the bottle of water. He couldn't deny the truth behind Nico's words. Elijah's dream had been to become one of the best pastry chefs in the world. And he had achieved this, at an age when most were still struggling to make themselves recognized on the international scene.

But his aspirations had changed over time. And everything he wanted was right here, in the town where he was born. The bakery he and his beloved grandmother had once longed for. The little girl who had won over his heart with her charm and sweet smiles.

And the remarkable man he had fallen in love with.

CARTER LOOKED AROUND WHEN ELIJAH WALKED INSIDE his kitchen a few hours later.

"Hey." Elijah walked over to where Carter sat drinking a cup of coffee at the island. "How's our princess?"

Carter smiled and kissed him, his tension melting away. He'd been worried about Elijah's absence and tried his best not to show it.

"Her fever's come down already. She asked for you a while back."

Elijah made a face. "I'm sorry I missed that. I'll pop my head in her room in a bit."

Carter observed Elijah's preoccupied expression for a moment before climbing off the stool and wrapping his arms around him. He knew Elijah still felt remorseful about the fact that Maisie had fallen ill while they had been making out at his place.

Elijah stiffened in surprise before returning the hug. "What was that for?"

"You look like you needed it." Carter breathed in Elijah's clean scent, shocked that it immediately soothed him. "God, I know it's only been a few hours, but I've missed you!"

Elijah chuckled in Carter's shoulder. "I've missed you too. And you were right, I needed that hug."

Carter pulled back and narrowed his eyes. "Did Nico say something?"

Elijah hesitated. "He did. But he's not going to make me change my mind. About getting back together with him or about going to Paris. This is where I belong."

Elijah's words echoed between them. Carter couldn't help but feel that he'd meant more than just Twilight Falls. Elijah's warmth seeped into Carter's flesh and bones. Desire stirred inside him.

It took everything Carter had to step away from the alluring pastry chef.

"So, what's for dinner?" he said in a light voice.

Elijah grinned, oblivious to the lustful direction Carter's thoughts had just taken. "Maisie's favorite. French hot dogs and fries."

Maisie woke up long enough to have some food before falling back to sleep. Elijah helped Carter clean up and accepted his offer of a nightcap. They sat on the back porch and sipped at their brandy while they chatted in low voices.

"So, filming starts next week?" Elijah said.

"Yeah." Carter grimaced. "It's a sequel to last year's

summer blockbuster, so the stunts are gonna be even more grueling."

Interest sparked in Elijah's eyes. "Is that why you've been spending so much time working out lately?"

"Yup. Hunter has a private gym at the back of his store. The studio sent me the training program for the movie. I've been spending a couple of hours at his place every morning." Carter flexed his left bicep. "By the time this project is over, I'm gonna be so buff, you might not recognize me."

Elijah blinked.

Carter's heart sank at his absorbed expression. "Wait. Don't tell me you like muscular macho guys?!"

"No!" Elijah protested. He paused and pursed his lips. "I love your body just the way it is, but I can't help but be curious."

Carter did his best not to preen at the compliment. "Well, I'm sorry to disappoint you, but my dick's not gonna get bigger."

Elijah burst out laughing.

They headed back inside a short while later. Carter escorted Elijah to the front door and had just stepped in the foyer when Elijah grabbed his hand and pulled him to a stop.

"This will do."

Carter gazed at him, puzzled. His pulse stuttered when Elijah shot him a sexy smile, pushed him against the wall, and dropped to his knees in front of him. "What are you—?" He stopped and sucked in air when Elijah nibbled on his cock through his jeans.

"Lunch and dinner were great, but there's something I've been dying to put in my mouth all day." Elijah's heated gaze stayed on Carter's face as he unbuckled Carter's belt and popped open the top button of his jeans.

Carter clenched his hands against the wall while Elijah tantalizingly pulled his zipper down. He groaned when his stiffening cock sprung free a heartbeat later.

Elijah didn't waste any time going after what he wanted. He wrapped one hand around Carter's shaft and teased his growing length with his fingers and hot flicks of his tongue until he brought him to a full erection.

Elijah gave Carter little warning before swallowing his rock-hard dick all the way to the back of his throat in one fell swoop.

"Fuck!" Carter brought a fist to his mouth and bit down on his flesh to drown his grunts of pleasure as Elijah started sucking and deep-throating him.

Elijah played with Carter's balls before skimming a hand under his T-shirt and across his twitching belly. He gave a particularly powerful suck and pressed the heel of his hand below Carter's navel.

An insane bolt of ecstasy slammed into Carter, drawing a muffled shout from his throat and causing one hand to drop to Elijah's head, his fingers clutching Elijah's hair desperately. He shivered and convulsed, aware that he was experiencing a dry orgasm.

Elijah carried on working Carter's twitching length expertly with his fingers and his mouth. Carter finally exploded at the back of Elijah's mouth with a harsh, muted cry, his swollen cock pulsing and filling Elijah's greedy throat with his hot cum.

CHAPTER TWENTY-FOUR

CARTER WIPED HIS SWEAT-SOAKED FACE WITH A TOWEL and turned to the stunt man who'd been working beside him.

"Thanks, Grant. That was a great scene!"

The stuntman grinned before giving him a playful slap on the back. "It's a pleasure, as always. I was worried you wouldn't be able to keep up with Francis's training program since you were working out on your own, but I see you're as dedicated as ever." His gaze shifted to the edge of the area where they'd been filming. "And your niece is as good as gold." His expression grew more serious. "I heard you had a terrible time with her at the beginning, but you couldn't tell that now. You've done a great job of settling her in, Carter."

Carter observed Maisie proudly where she sat in a fake director's chair his assistant had provided for her, her eyes sparkling with interest as she observed the people on set. "I have many people to thank for that."

He'd gotten permission from the studio to have Maisie come over today and was relieved she hadn't gotten bored. With his niece scheduled to start preschool tomorrow, Carter knew he would miss their days together sorely and wanted to make the most of the time they had left.

Carter had been surprised by the open expressions of support he'd received since he turned up on set for the first day of filming a week ago. It seemed the story of how he'd become the guardian to his niece and moved from L.A. for her sake had resonated with many of his co-workers.

He masked a grimace.

That will probably change when I come out of the closet.

Now that he'd committed to his relationship with Elijah, Carter was determined to embrace the challenges still to come, including the PR storm that would break out when he declared his bisexuality to the world. He knew he would be putting his career on the line and that it might mean the end of his astounding success to date, but he was confident he could weather the hardship with Elijah and his friends at his side. And Carter owed it to Maisie to be open and honest about every aspect of his life. Especially now that he'd decided to start official proceedings to adopt her as his daughter.

Elijah had been the first person he'd confessed his plans to, in bed the night before. With Maisie in the house, they weren't openly amorous with one another and had taken to keeping their intimate moments to a time when she would be asleep, Elijah making sure he left the house before Maisie woke up in the morning. Although Carter was grateful for Elijah's consideration for his niece, he missed greeting the day with the pastry chef snuggled up in his arms.

Elijah had thoroughly encouraged his decision to adopt Maisie.

"I can't think of a better thing." Elijah kissed Carter, his eyes shining with excitement. "Maisie will be so thrilled!"

Carter hesitated. "She might think I'm trying to replace her parents."

Elijah shook his head. "Maisie adores you. And you love her. You'll make a great dad, Carter. You're one helluva an amazing guy."

"You're pretty amazing yourself, you know that?" Carter trailed gentle fingers down Elijah's cheek where they lay facing each other on their sides, their heads on the same pillow. "Maisie and I wouldn't have gotten this far without you."

Elijah flushed enchantingly. "You're exaggerating."

"I'm not." Carter moved his hand down Elijah's body and leaned over to nibble on his earlobe. "And sex with you is out of this world."

Elijah shuddered.

Carter stroked Elijah's stirring cock with his knuckles and pushed him onto his back.

"You have to be at the studio in eight hours," Elijah protested mildly as Carter reached for the box of condoms on the nightstand.

"I know." Carter sheathed himself and spread Elijah's thighs open. "But you are—" he aligned his cock with Elijah's

softened entrance and slid home in a single thrust, drawing a throaty gasp from Elijah, "pretty irresistible."

Elijah wrapped his legs and arms around Carter as Carter started making love to him, their gasps and moans and groans muffled between their lips.

Though Nico had started spending more time in L.A. to concentrate on his new business venture, Carter and Elijah's nighttime arrangements had not escaped the attention of the Michelin star chef.

Carter's assistant, a pretty blonde with blue eyes, sauntered over, Maisie holding on to her hand. Carter had sensed the blonde's interest in him, but had made it clear from his interactions with her that he intended to keep things professional. In another life, he would have accepted her advances and slept with her after filming ended.

The only person Carter was interested in having sex with these days was a captivating chef with chocolate brown hair and eyes.

"We're done for the day," his assistant said. "Filming starts at lunchtime tomorrow, so you can sleep in." She turned to Maisie and dropped down on her haunches. "Enjoy school, Maisie. I'm sure you'll have a great time."

Maisie nodded. She opened the coloring book she had in her hold and shyly offered a sheet to Carter's assistant. "Here, I made this for you."

Carter's assistant eyes widened as she beheld the drawing, her pleasure evident. "Oh wow. Thank you, Maisie." She gave the little girl a hug.

Maisie blushed.

"Well, isn't this nice?" someone drawled behind Carter.

Carter stiffened before slowly turning around.

Mira had walked onto the set and stood staring at them.

Carter's assistant paled. She rose to her feet. "See you tomorrow, Mr. Wilson." She nodded stiffly at Mira, said goodbye to Maisie, and headed briskly away.

Mira followed her with her gaze, her expression cool. "She's definitely interested in you." She looked at Carter. "Does she know?"

Carter eyed her coldly. "Does she know what?"

Mira arched an eyebrow. "The thing we talked about the last time we met. Your preferences in—" she glanced at Maisie, "*partners.*"

Tiny hands clasped Carter's leg. He looked down and saw that Maisie had stepped behind him, her gaze wary as she stared up at Mira.

"Hello," Mira said, injecting some warmth into her voice. She leaned down and extended a manicured hand to Carter's niece. "You must be Maisie. I'm Mira."

Maisie hesitated. "Hello," she mumbled in a small voice. She did not shake Mira's hand.

Carter could have kissed Maisie then.

Mira straightened, her expression growing cool once more. She turned to Carter. "Have you given any thought to my offer?"

"I haven't," Carter said in a dead voice. "I gave you my answer that day. It hasn't changed."

Mira's eyes flashed with anger. Carter stood his ground.

"Fine," Mira snapped. "Don't say I didn't warn you." She twisted on her heels and stormed off.

Unease filtered through Carter at he watched his former lover disappear from the set. He was still thinking about what Mira had said when he drove back to Twilight Falls a short time later. Elijah was waiting for them when they got home.

"It's Mac and cheese tonight," the chef said with a warm smile as Carter and Maisie entered the kitchen.

Carter had given Elijah a spare key to his home so he could come and go at will.

"Uncle Elijah!" Maisie bolted across the room and hugged Elijah's leg tightly. "I had so much fun today! Uncle Carter was amazing!"

Elijah ruffled her hair and pressed a kiss to the top of her head. "I'm sure he was, honey. Want to change before dinner?"

Maisie nodded vigorously before running out of the room.

Carter came over and looped his arms around Elijah's waist. "Don't I get a kiss too?"

Elijah pressed a hand against Carter's mouth as he leaned in to take his lips. "Patience."

Carter narrowed his eyes and nibbled on Elijah's fingertips. "I think this deserves some kind of punishment later."

Elijah shivered, lust sparking in his brown eyes. Carter had discovered that Elijah very much enjoyed domination play. He was particularly partial to the red silk tie Carter had used the first night they'd made love and had asked Carter to blindfold him on several occasions. The way Elijah's hole gripped Carter's cock when he braced himself on all fours while Carter plunged inside him from behind told Carter exactly how much he'd relished that particular bondage game. And Carter had to admit that experiencing Elijah's total submission was pretty intoxicating.

They had dinner, put Maisie to bed, and headed into Carter's bedroom, their hands intertwined. Carter undressed the both of them before taking the silk tie from the nightstand and tying it around Elijah's eyes. Elijah trembled as Carter pushed him down on the bed, his erection already leaking precum.

Carter climbed in after Elijah and straddled his body. He stared, mesmerized, at the expanse of beautiful skin and toned muscles spread out beneath him. The way Elijah licked his lips and his chest moved with his ragged breathing told Carter just how excited he was right now.

Carter smiled, shuffled down the bed, and blew air softly over Elijah's dick.

Elijah hissed and bit his lower lip, his hips pumping off the sheets in anticipation of what was to come. Carter closed his fingers around Elijah's cock, took him inside his mouth, and blew him to an orgasm. Elijah was still shuddering with aftershocks of pleasure when Carter flipped him on his front. Carter pulled Elijah onto his hands and knees, his heart thudding rapidly, his own erection now raging.

Elijah's head dropped forward as Carter spread his

butt cheeks. He stiffened when Carter pressed a hungry kiss to his pucker. Carter furrowed his tongue and went to town on Elijah's twitching hole.

CHAPTER TWENTY-FIVE

Dawn was breaking when they tip-toed down the stairs the next morning, Carter insisting on walking Elijah to the front door.

"I'll see you tonight?" Carter said in a hopeful voice. He shivered as the cool air washed across his bare chest.

"Sure. Now get inside before you catch a cold."

Carter smiled at Elijah's husky voice. He'd had Elijah stifling his screams of pleasure for a good couple of hours before they'd fallen asleep in a tangle of sweaty arms and legs.

Elijah sighed. "Ten dollars say I can guess what you're thinking about right now."

Carter's smile widened. "I suspect you would win that bet." He leaned in and dropped a quick peck on Elijah's cheek. "See you tonight, my love muffin."

Elijah arched an eyebrow, his expression haughty. "Love muffin?" He glanced down at his lean body and defined abs. "Are you saying I've put weight on?"

Carter chuckled before slipping an arm around Elijah's waist. He bent a surprised Elijah backward at the waist and took his mouth in a slow, deep kiss.

"I would love you even if you were fat, old, and gray, Elijah Davis," Carter said against Elijah's lips when he ended the torrid exchange.

Elijah's eyes widened.

Carter waited breathlessly for Elijah's response to his impromptu confession, his pulse thrumming rapidly in his veins.

Elijah's fingers shook slightly as he brought his hands to Carter's face, his expression sobering. "And I would love you if you were fat, old, and gray, Carter Wilson." He pressed his forehead against Carter's before taking Carter's mouth in a kiss full of promise.

Carter's heart soared dizzyingly.

A faint noise broke through his joyous daze. He stiffened when he looked past Elijah's shoulder.

A car he didn't recognize was parked at the end of the cul-de-sac, beyond Elijah's house. A figure sat behind the steering wheel. It put something away, started the engine, and drove off rapidly.

Carter wrenched his mouth from Elijah's and scowled. "Shit."

Elijah startled at Carter's curse. "Carter?" He turned and gazed at the vehicle disappearing down the road, his expression puzzled. "What's wrong?"

Carter clenched his fists as he recalled Mira's words from the day before.

That bitch!

"That was a reporter."

Elijah paled. "Did he see us?"

Although Carter knew his world was about to be rocked by the mother of all scandals, he felt strangely calm. The moment he'd long dreaded was finally upon him and it wasn't as bad as he'd feared it would be. He slipped his cell out of the back pocket of his jeans and took Elijah's hand.

"Yes. And I'm pretty sure he took pictures." Carter hit his agent's number and brought his phone to his ear, his fingers tightening around Elijah's while he gazed at him, his expression determined. "You may want to skip work today. This will likely make showbiz headlines by lunch time."

"HOW BADLY DO YOU WANT TO DISAPPEAR RIGHT NOW?" Sam chewed her lower lip anxiously as she scrolled through a media outlet's newsfeed on her cell. She was on her break, Daisy and the new assistant manager and waiter they'd hired a couple of weeks back holding the fort out front.

Elijah looked up from where he was making a fresh batch of macaroons and glanced at the swing door leading to the shop. A low roar of voices came from beyond it.

The place was packed even more than usual considering it was a week day.

To say that he was stunned by how rapidly the story and pictures of a bare-chested Carter kissing a mystery man on his front porch had spread on social media would be an understatement. Though Carter had done his best to prepare Elijah for what would happen when he came out of the closet, Elijah couldn't help be apprehensive.

He knew his bakery business was unlikely to suffer significantly from the fallout of this scandal. The ones he was most concerned about were Carter and Maisie.

It was Maisie's first day at preschool. Elijah was due to pick her up in a couple of hours and babysit her at the bakery until Carter got home. Carter had given the preschool a list of the people who could be contacted in case of an emergency while he was off shooting his movie. Elijah's phone number had joined Izzy's and the Terrible Seven a week ago.

He glanced at his cell where it lay on the counter to his left.

So far, the preschool hadn't called him.

"Elijah?" Sam frowned. "You okay?"

Elijah put the tray of macaroons in the oven and turned to face her. "Not really." He sighed. "And the answer to your question is no, I don't want to go anywhere. My place is by Carter's side."

Sam's eyes widened slightly. "Wow. Things really are serious between the two of you, huh?"

"They always were. From the very beginning."

A hulking figure marched through the swing door.

Armando, their new waiter and assistant shop manager, cracked his knuckles. "Do you have insurance?" he asked Elijah grimly.

Elijah blinked. "Yes. Why?"

"Because some asshole reporter just upset Daisy

and I want him to taste my wrath," Armando ground out.

"Whoa there, hot stuff." Sam dropped a heavy hand on the high school quarterback's shoulder even though he towered above her. "Let's not be hasty. Violence isn't the answer to anything."

A loud crash came from the direction of the shop. They jumped before turning and storming through the swing door, Elijah bringing up the rear with a scowl on his face.

"All right, violence *may* be the answer to some things," Sam ground out between clenched teeth.

Daisy stood ashen-faced in the middle of the shop, a tray of broken cups at her feet. A man was holding a voice-recorder in the waitress's face, his expression shining with overzealousness.

"Have you seen Mr. Davis and Mr. Wilson engage in overt sexual acts in the workplace?"

Elijah marched over to the reporter while Sam and Armando led a shocked Daisy away. "Get out of my shop, right now!"

Stunned silence fell across the crammed bakery as Elijah's roar echoed across the room. The reporter blinked. A camera flashed on Elijah's left.

He glared at the woman who'd taken the picture. "I would be grateful if you could leave too."

"Or what?" the male reporter said defiantly.

Elijah turned to Sam. "Phone the police."

Murmurs broke out around the shop. Elijah felt dozens of hot stares on his face.

The attention should have made him balk. Yet, he

had never felt as righteous as he did in that moment. He was fighting this battle not just for himself, but for his future with Carter and Maisie.

A low clapping started at the back of the shop. Elijah startled.

An elderly woman had risen to her feet and was putting her hands together in an enthusiastic expression of appreciation. Others followed and half the shop was soon on their feet.

"That's right!" someone shouted. "Ain't nobody's business what the chef and the movie star get up to. It's their lives!"

"You should be ashamed of yourselves," the elderly lady said grumpily as she came forward with her walking stick. She raised her cane and tapped the male reporter in the chest with the sharp end. "Why, I have known those two boys and their families their entire lives and I can tell you one thing: they are both honorable men from what I have seen."

Elijah stared. "Mrs. Finch? Is that you?!"

The elderly dame turned and smiled at Elijah. "I'm glad you finally recognized your old homeroom teacher. You may not know this, but I took up correspondence with your grandmother when she came to visit that one time. I was sorry to hear about her passing away. She would be so proud of all that you've achieved since you came back to Twilight Falls."

Elijah's eyes rounded. "I—I didn't know that."

"So, was Mr. Davis openly gay when he was in high school?" the female reporter piped up. She raising her camera at Elijah's homeroom teacher.

Elijah narrowed his eyes. Before he could go over and escort her and the male reporter to the door, someone stepped forward.

"You people really take the biscuit."

Everyone turned to the fearsome redhead walking up to the female reporter. The stranger took a firm hold of the woman's arm and drew her to her feet.

"Hey!" The reporter scowled. "What do you think you're doing?!"

"Officer Marigold." The redhead flashed a badge at the female reporter. "I may be off duty right now, but that doesn't stop me from wanting to arrest your ass for disorderly conduct." The policeman turned to Elijah. "Is that stud muffin from Paris still around? 'Cause I sure would like to taste one of his savory pastries again."

Laughter broke out around the bakery.

Elijah's lips curved in a slow smile. "I'm sure I can convince him to make some more."

"Deal." The policewoman took the male reporter's arm and guided the two journalists to the front door. "I'll tell you paparazzi something now. Don't mess with one of our own. This town won't take that kind of shit lying down."

CHAPTER TWENTY-SIX

"I mean, come on! It's the 21st century. Gay sex shouldn't be making headline news anymore."

Carter stared at the TV on the wall of his personal trailer.

A popular talk show was being aired and the topic of conversation was one Carter Wilson. Grainy pictures of him kissing Elijah on his front porch that morning were pasted all over the studio backdrop.

"They sure are relishing this, aren't they?" Barbara murmured. She sat at the small dining table to his right, frantically fielding calls and emails.

"Have you heard from my lawyers yet?" Carter asked his agent in a hard voice.

"Yes. They'll be releasing your statement within the hour."

Carter's cell pinged in his hand. He looked at the screen and released a sigh of relief. Elijah had picked Maisie up from preschool and taken her to his home.

Carter stilled.

Did he close up early? It's not even four yet.

The mystery was resolved in the next moment. An excited uproar rose from the TV speakers, drawing Carter and Barbara's gazes.

"Folks, it seems we have some breaking news," the show host said above the chatter of the live audience. "Someone just released a video of Carter Wilson's apparent new flame."

Carter's stomach dropped when a clip started playing across the screen. It showed Elijah storming across his bakery and coldly requesting two reporters leave his shop. What happened next had the show's host and her guests and audience gasping, and Carter's jaw sagging open.

He sat down shakily next to Barbara and watched as practically the entire shop rose to their feet to defend Elijah. A grin split his mouth when he recognized the elderly woman who launched into a tirade against a male reporter as his old homeroom teacher. The show host and the studio audience chuckled at Officer Marigold's timely intervention. The clip ended with a shot of the off-duty police officer escorting the reporters out of *La Petite Bouche Gourmande*.

"Well, there you have it. Our mystery man." The show's host turned to her guests where they sat at the breakfast bar that served as the main seating area. "What did you ladies think of that?"

"Carter Wilson has great taste in men," one of the women said bluntly. She was an actress who'd played a supporting role in one of Carter's movies and they'd grown to respect one other as work colleagues over the years.

The audience roared and started clapping. Wolf-whistles broke out above the din.

"They love him," Barbara said with a smile. "That will work in our favor."

Carter frowned.

The agent sighed. "Don't look at me like that. You're the one responsible for this shitstorm. It's my job to salvage what remains of your career."

Someone knocked on the door of the trailer. Carter made to rise to his feet.

Barbara stopped him. "Let me. It could be a reporter. Those assholes are notorious for getting past studio security."

It wasn't a reporter.

"Can I come in?" the man on the doorstep said somberly.

Carter's heart sank at his cool expression.

What he'd feared the most was already unfolding.

ELIJAH GLANCED AT THE CLOCK IN THE KITCHEN. IT WAS past seven thirty and Carter still hadn't come home. He suppressed the nervous tension swirling through him and checked the oven.

The beef and vegetable casserole he'd prepared for their dinner was almost ready.

"That smells yummy, Uncle Elijah," Maisie said.

"Thank you." Elijah turned to where she perched on

a chair at the kitchen table, her legs dangling off the floor. She was doodling in the new coloring book the preschool had given her that day.

A wave of affection washed over him as he studied the little girl. He knew Carter was making the right decision adopting her.

A tiny frown suddenly appeared on Maisie's brow. She stopped coloring and looked up at him. "Uncle Elijah, what does it mean to have two daddies?"

Elijah startled. He hesitated before walking slowly over to the table and taking the seat next to Maisie.

The little girl continued looking at him with a puzzled expression, unaware of his pounding heart.

"Did someone say something to you, Maisie?" Elijah asked carefully.

"One of the teachers was talking about Uncle Carter and a," she pulled a face as she struggled to pronounce her next word, "—a mysty man. She said I was going to have two daddies and that she felt sorry for me."

Shit. Elijah silently cursed the gossipy staff at Maisie's preschool.

"But then this boy at school told me having two daddies was fun." Maisie's eyes sparkled. "He has two daddies and a mommy. And there was a girl who has two mommies."

Elijah blessed the honesty of children. He moved from the chair to kneel next to the little girl. "Would you like that, Maisie?" he said gently. "Having two daddies?"

Maisie put her coloring pen down, her tiny face

growing serious. She stared at her hands and fiddled nervously with her fingers, her blue eyes darkening with some nameless emotion.

Elijah's heart faltered. *I shouldn't have asked her that.*

"I'm sorry, sweet—"

"I know *Maman et Papa* are in Heaven," Maisie said in a small voice. "And I know Uncle Carter said I will see them again one day, when I go to Heaven too." She looked up at Elijah, her eyes slowly filling with tears. "But I want Uncle Carter to be *mon papa*. I really, really want that!"

Elijah swallowed the lump in his throat and wrapped the little girl in his arms.

"Uncle Carter wants that too, honey." He pressed a loving kiss in Maisie's hair. "He really wants to call you his *petite fille*."

Maisie's fingers tightened on Elijah's back. "He does?!"

Elijah pulled back and wiped a hasty hand across his wet eyes before looking into Maisie's stunned face. He smiled shakily and nodded. "Yes, *ma puce*."

The biggest grin in the world split Maisie's mouth. She let out a squeal of excitement and hugged Elijah again.

"Will you be *mon papa* too, Elijah?!"

Elijah stilled, shocked by the unexpected question.

Maisie looked up at him. "Uncle Carter really likes you. And you are always at our house." She wrinkled her nose. "And you and Uncle Carter do secret smoochies, just like *Maman et Papa* used to do when they thought I wasn't looking."

Elijah flushed. *Oh God.*

However much he wanted to sink into a hole in the ground right now, he knew there was no escaping Maisie's question. He stroked Maisie's head and gazed into her bright eyes, knowing that the words he was about to utter were an honest expression of the sweet feelings that had taken root inside him in the past few weeks.

"If you and Carter will have me, then yes, I would love to be your *Papa* too, Maisie."

Maisie squealed and hugged Elijah again.

Elijah's cell vibrated in his back pocket. He slipped it out and frowned when he saw a number he didn't recognize lighting up the screen. He was about to decline the call when something made him hesitate.

Elijah's finger hovered above the answer button for a moment. He rose to his feet and finally accepted the call.

"Hello?"

"Is that Elijah?" a woman asked briskly.

"It is," Elijah replied cautiously. "Who is this?"

"I'm Barbara Coombs, Carter's agent. I've just taken him to his home in Malibu. I take it you've seen the showbiz headlines today?"

Dread pooled inside Elijah. "Yeah, I have."

"Well, so did a bunch of studio executives. They dropped Carter from the movie this afternoon."

Elijah froze. "What?!"

Maisie stared at him anxiously.

"Hang on a minute," Elijah said curtly in the phone before turning to Maisie. "It's okay, sweetheart." He forced a smile on his face. "I'm gonna take this call outside."

Maisie nodded and returned to her coloring. Elijah stepped out into the hallway.

"Elijah, you there?"

"Yeah, I'm here." Elijah clenched his teeth. He couldn't even begin to imagine the state Carter must be in. What the actor had feared the most was happening. "How's Carter?"

"He's calmed down a bit."

Elijah's heart twisted in pain. "Was—was he that upset?"

"Oh, you misunderstand me. He wasn't distressed. He was angry. It took me and his lawyers two hours to calm him now. He wants to sue Mira and the studio."

Elijah's eyes rounded. "He wants to do what?!"

"His lawyers were going to release the statement he'd prepared about coming out this afternoon, but we've decided to hang fire and review our game plan after he sleeps on it. That's why I took him to Malibu. He doesn't want Maisie to see him in this state. He also wants the paparazzi's focus away from you and his niece for the next twenty-four hours. There's a bunch of them parked outside his place right now. He intended to call you but someone got hold of his private number while we were still at his lawyers and the network's locked it down for the next twelve hours. All his calls are being directed to me."

A storm of emotions raged through Elijah as he absorbed what Carter's agent had just told him. He swallowed. "Can you give me Carter's address?"

"I don't think that's a good idea," Barbara said after a pause.

"It may not be, but Carter needs us right now." Elijah fisted his hands. "He needs Maisie and me."

Nico came through the front door just as Elijah ended the call.

"There's a couple of news vans outside," the French chef said in a disgruntled voice. "They practically followed me to the door." He frowned when he saw Elijah's expression. "Are you okay? I heard the news."

Elijah nodded. "I'm fine. I have a favor to ask you."

CHAPTER TWENTY-SEVEN

CARTER GAZED MOODILY OUT AT THE PHOSPHORESCENT surf crashing on the shoreline before taking a sip of whisky. The anger he'd felt all afternoon had finally abated.

The face of the studio executive who'd come to his trailer swam before his eyes. Carter's fingers tightened on his glass. He forced himself to take a calming breath.

I can't believe those assholes had the audacity to do that!

Carter knew he had grounds to sue the studio and Mira for defamation and breach of contract. His lawyers had agreed with him on those points. But they'd also warned him that going to war with the studio could mean the end of his career.

"My career's already ended," Carter said brusquely as he paced the floor.

Barbara frowned. "You don't know that."

"Who the hell would want to hire a gay action movie star, Barbara?! It's not exactly as if this industry is famed for being open-minded!"

Tense silence fell across the conference room.

Carter fisted his hands, conscious he'd gone too far. "I'm sorry. That was uncalled for."

"Apology accepted," the older woman said with a curt nod.

"We've managed clients through worse scandals than this," one of his lawyers said calmly. "Being gay is no longer the shocking news it used to be."

Another lawyer sighed at Carter's skeptical expression. "Okay, so your case is more complicated. You're a major movie star with millions of female fans all over the world and have a reputation as Hollywood's number one Casanova. I know you feel your fans will be disappointed by today's events, but I think you'll be surprised by how many will come out to support you and condemn the studio for their action today. I suggest you sleep on things for one night. We can talk in the morning." He paused. "If you still feel strongly about it, then we'll start court proceedings against the studio and Mira."

A door slammed somewhere in the house. Carter turned and spied one of his bodyguards walking into the lounge from the front hall.

The security company Barbara had hired to guard Carter for the next forty-eight hours was one they'd used before, at his U.S. premieres. Carter trusted the men to make sure that the paparazzi didn't enter the grounds of his home.

"Everything okay?"

The bodyguard nodded. "Yes. There's a van at the gate. It's got the logo of a sports apparel shop on the side. The guy driving it said he's got a delivery for you. He said to tell you his name was Nico."

Carter's eyes widened. *What the—?*

"Let him in."

The van was pulling around the side of his house when Carter rushed outside. He watched the driver step out, his pulse racing.

"Nico? What's going on?"

The French chef frowned. "I can't believe I'm helping my enemy. You owe me for this, Wilson." He grabbed the handle of the van's side door and pulled it open.

Maisie shot out of her seat and launched herself in his arms. "Uncle Carter! Surprise!"

Carter's heart lifted, the dark clouds that had shrouded him all day dissipating in a flood of emotions.

Elijah stepped out after her, a tentative smile on his face. "Hey."

Carter closed the distance between them, wrapped a hand around the back of Elijah's head, and took his mouth in a passionate kiss, heedless of the bodyguards watching them and an incensed-looking Nico.

"That's a big smoochie," Maisie mumbled.

Carter froze. He'd forgotten he was still holding his niece. He took his mouth off Elijah's and looked woefully at the little girl. "I'm—I'm sorry, Maisie. You—"

"She knows." Elijah flushed under their audience's gazes. "About us."

"Uncle Carter likes smooching Uncle Elijah lots," Maisie stated with a definitive nod.

Heat flooded Carter's face. *I'm definitely gonna have to ask him about this later.*

Carter's attention moved to the van. "That's Hunter's, isn't it?"

"Yeah." Elijah rubbed the back of his neck. "There are reporters outside my house. I thought it would be best if they didn't see us leave. Hunter was more than happy to lend us the vehicle. It was a bit tricky getting to it from the back porch, but Nico helped."

Carter turned to the French chef. "Thank you."

"This doesn't mean I've accepted you," Nico muttered irritably. "You're still my love rival."

Carter sighed. "You really don't know when to give up, do you?"

CHAPTER TWENTY-EIGHT

Elijah watched as Carter quietly pulled Maisie's bedroom door shut, leaving a narrow gap. It was past eleven and they'd just managed to settle the little girl down. They headed down the stairs and into the kitchen, Elijah glancing curiously around the place.

Carter's modern Malibu mansion was as far removed from his cozy home in Twilight Falls as the sun was from the moon.

"Coffee?" Carter indicated the sleek machine on the counter.

Elijah shook his head. "No, thanks. I'm too hyped up for caffeine."

"I know just what you need."

Carter took Elijah into the lounge, poured them a shot of whisky from the minibar, and guided him to the terrace.

"Wow." Elijah stopped and stared at the breathtaking view stretched out beyond the balcony. "That's quite something to come home to."

The corner of Carter's mouth tilted in a half-smile. "Better than Twilight Falls?"

Elijah hesitated before shaking his head. "Nothing will ever beat Twilight Falls."

They stepped to the edge of the deck and gazed at the star-dotted sky above the dark ocean.

"I'm sorry you got dropped from the movie," Elijah said quietly.

His body felt strangely light again, as if a huge weight had lifted off his shoulders. He knew it was Carter's presence that had finally gotten him to relax for the first time that day, the turbulent feelings that had been simmering inside him fading away.

Carter sighed and turned to lean his back against the railing. "And I'm sorry about what happened at your shop today." A low chuckle passed his lips. "Mrs. Finch was amazing."

Elijah smiled. "She sure told them."

A comfortable silence fell between them.

"I'm still angry about how they shut me down," Carter said. "I knew this wouldn't be easy, but I didn't think they'd cancel an active project."

"Do your lawyers think you have a case against the studio?"

"Yeah, they do." Carter made a face. "But they've also warned me against it."

"Because they think you might lose?"

"Because I will lose whichever way the dice falls. If I win in court, I will be labeled a contentious actor and few studios will want to touch me. If I lose, it will be a landmark case that will have an everlasting impact on

Hollywood and the acting world. It will erode at the rights of every performer in this town and give the studios an open license to hire and fire us at will."

Elijah sobered at that. He hadn't thought beyond Carter's situation and how the events of today could affect an entire industry.

"What will you do?"

"I'm going to sleep on it, like they told me to."

Elijah stayed quiet for a while as he gazed out over the ocean. "Maisie said something to me tonight."

"She did?" Carter said.

"She wants you to be her father."

Elijah turned to see Carter staring at him, visibly shocked. He explained what had happened at Maisie's preschool and the conversation he'd had with the little girl that evening.

Emotion darkened Carter's eyes, causing them to glisten. He put their glasses on a table, wrapped his arms around Elijah, and burrowed his face in Elijah's neck. Elijah hugged him tightly, his heart clenching when he felt the wetness of tears against his skin.

They stayed like that for a long time, their pounding hearts echoing against each other's chest.

"Will you marry me?"

Elijah's eyes rounded at Carter's thick words.

Carter lifted his head and gazed hotly at Elijah. "Marry me, Elijah."

Elijah's vision blurred.

"I—" He cradled Carter's face in his hands and looked at him anxiously, the thought that had been festering at the back of his mind since Carter first declared his love for him finally finding voice. "Are you sure? You're bi, Carter. You may still find a woman you'll fall in love with—"

"I will never love another person the way I love you, Elijah. Man or woman."

Elijah's heart soared at the truth blazing in Carter's eyes. He pressed a heartfelt kiss to Carter's mouth. "Ask me again."

Carter swallowed, his expression sobering. "Will you marry me, Elijah Davis?"

"Yes," Elijah whispered against Carter's lips, his eyes locked on Carter's.

Carter shuddered. Sparks flashed between them as he deepened their kiss, his tongue slipping inside Elijah's mouth to claim his flesh in a bold, commanding dance.

Elijah's pulse accelerated. "Carter," he sighed when Carter finally lifted his mouth off his, the heat smoldering between them causing his breath to catch.

Elijah was already hard by the time Carter led him upstairs and into his bedroom. Carter pulled the curtains closed and switched on a pair of soft-glowing night lamps. He yanked his T-shirt over his head and dropped it on the floor before stripping rapidly out of his jeans and boxers, his hooded gaze locked on Elijah's. He moved toward Elijah, his expression predatory.

Elijah's heart raced wildly as he stared at Carter's honed muscles and tanned skin. He could see the results of Carter's intense training from the way he'd beefed up slightly in his limbs, and the defined six-pack and deep V arrowing to his groin.

"I believe one of us has too many clothes on." Carter stopped in front of Elijah, hooked a finger in the neckline of his T-shirt, and tugged him close.

Elijah smiled. "I can see how that could be a problem." His gaze dropped to Carter's impressive erection. He stroked a knuckle down Carter's shaft and grinned when Carter let out a low curse.

Carter wasted no time undressing Elijah, his movements almost clumsy in his haste. Elijah chuckled. Then he gasped.

Carter had closed one hand around his cock and given him a slick rub.

Carter stroked Elijah until he was humming in pleasure and clutching at Carter's shoulders, his toes curling in the carpet. He let go of Elijah's trembling dick, took Elijah's hand, and guided him across the room.

Elijah's eyes widened when they passed the bed. "Where are we going?"

"There's something I've been wanting to do for a while now."

Carter flashed Elijah a sexy smile and tugged him inside a spacious bathroom.

Elijah's eyes widened when he saw the enormous, dark Italian marble rainfall shower. "Oh."

Carter arched an eyebrow. "I hope you'll be saying more than that by the time we're done in here."

Elijah flushed. Carter pulled him inside the open

shower, turned the water on, and took his face in his hands, his lips desperate as he kissed Elijah. Elijah gripped the back of Carter's head, the sensation of Carter's wet skin and his hungry tongue so heady his legs threatened to give way beneath him.

CHAPTER TWENTY-NINE

Carter wrenched his mouth from Elijah's and rained smoldering kisses down his throat and chest, his tongue flicking Elijah's stiff nipples and drawing gasps from him.

"Have I told how delicious you taste?" Carter growled. He lowered himself to his knees and stroked his hands all the way down the sides of Elijah's ribcage to his waist and hips, his hot mouth finding Elijah's trembling belly. "All of you. Your lips. Your skin. Your dick. Your ass. I could feast on you all day and night."

Elijah's hands found Carter's hair when Carter closed his lips on the swollen head of his cock. Pleasure slammed into him at the first powerful suck of Carter's mouth. Carter moved his hands to Elijah's butt. He parted Elijah's crack, found his pucker, and circled and teased the twitching opening with the tip of a finger.

"Carter," Elijah moaned.

He looked down into Carter's passionate gaze and

almost came at the fiery light burning in the hazel depths.

Carter kept his eyes on Elijah as he started blowing him, his cheeks bulging with every motion of his head, his lips plump and slick with Elijah's precum. He pushed his finger inside Elijah and started thrusting.

"Oh!"

Elijah's hips jerked forward reflexively, sliding his cock deep inside Carter's eager mouth all the way to the back of his throat. Blood buzzed in Elijah's ears, drowning out the sound of running water and the sinful noises Carter's mouth was making on his dick. Waves of pleasure surged through him from his front and back end, Carter's sweet assault overwhelming his senses. Carter slipped a second finger inside him, stretching his entrance and driving him crazy all over again.

"Carter! Carter!" Elijah chanted breathlessly as he gripped Carter's head and pumped his hips. He drove his painfully aroused cock in and out of Carter's mouth, powerless against his body's primal instincts.

His limbs and spine stiffened with the most delicious preorgasmic tension.

Elijah came with a tortured cry, his climax driving him on the balls of his feet, his desperate voice echoing around the bathroom. Shudders shook him from his head all to way to his toes.

Carter slipped his fingers out of Elijah's ass and wrapped his arms around Elijah's waist as Elijah slumped against him seconds later.

Elijah's labored breathing was audible above the rushing noise of water.

"That was—"

"Pretty amazing, right?" Carter murmured with a low chuckle. "Let me get a condom." He made to rise to his feet.

Elijah's hands tightened on Carter's shoulders, keeping him down. He flushed as he stared at Carter, his eyes silently pleading.

Understanding dawned on Carter's face. He dropped a scorching kiss on Elijah's aching belly and ran light fingers across his butt cheeks. "You don't want the condom?"

Elijah bit his lip and shook his head.

Carter's eyes grew feverish, the hunger inside them so fierce it threatened to consume Elijah. "Say it, Elijah. Tell me what you want."

Elijah's ass clenched at Carter's rough command. Carter didn't miss his reaction. He kept his gaze on Elijah's and teased his softened pucker with a finger.

"Say it."

Elijah swallowed, his heart thundering in his chest. He couldn't deny Carter. And the prospect of saying the words out loud had him so hot and bothered, his dick was already swelling with fresh arousal.

"I want you inside me, Carter. I want your raw cock."

Carter's expression turned feral.

"I want to feel you come inside me." Elijah shivered and held Carter's gaze unblinkingly. "I want to feel your cum filling my hole. Take me, Carter."

Carter growled. He spun Elijah around, pushed him against the wall, and parted his butt cheeks with strong hands. Elijah let out a low keen as Carter's tongue found his eager pucker.

Carter licked and rimmed his entrance for a delicious minute. Then he stretched Elijah's hole open with his thumbs, furrowed his tongue, and entered his passage with the tip, his lips closing snugly on Elijah's folds.

Air locked in Elijah's throat. "*Carter!*"

His left hand found Carter's head where Carter knelt behind him.

Carter grunted at his desperate touch. He stilled his tongue.

Elijah moaned, clenched his fingers in Carter's hair, and thrust his ass toward Carter's mouth. Carter growled and carried on eating him.

By the time Carter climbed to his feet, Elijah was dizzy with pleasure and clutching at the wall with both hands. His cock twitched from the second intense orgasm he'd just had, his fresh cum glistening on the wet floor as it was washed away.

Carter turned him around, his touch gentle despite the deep yearning lighting up his flushed face. He hooked his hands under Elijah's thighs, lifted him up against the wall, and wrapped his legs around his waist.

"Hang on to me."

Elijah obeyed Carter's command and looped his arms around Carter's nape, blood roaring in his veins.

Carter guided the tip of his trembling erection to Elijah's entrance.

They both groaned when Carter teased Elijah's pucker with slow circles of his leaking cock. Elijah bit his lip at the sinful feel of Carter's naked dick.

Carter finally pressed the tip of his raging arousal to Elijah's hole. He grabbed on to Elijah's ass, bowed his spine, and pushed in.

"*Oh God!*" Elijah squeezed his eyes shut, the pleasure of Carter's raw penetration sending lightning bolts shooting through his back passage.

"Shit!" Carter bit down on Elijah's right shoulder. "*You feel SO good!*"

The room faded around Elijah as Carter started fucking him, his powerful movements propelling his erection slickly in and out of Elijah's hole. Elijah panted and gasped and moaned as he gave his body over to the man he loved, trusting him to take them safely to the other side of their savage lovemaking. Carter's thrusts grew more forceful as he pounded into Elijah, his fingers biting into Elijah's flesh where he held on to him, his mouth open on labored grunts on Elijah's throat.

Fire pooled deep inside Elijah's belly, the flames rising and ebbing with every stab of Carter's cock inside his body. His spine and thighs slowly stiffened, his balls rising as his climax bore down on him.

"*Carter! Carter!*"

"Look at me!"

Elijah blinked his eyes dazedly. Carter had raised his head and was staring at him with a savage intensity, his lips parted on harsh breaths. He lowered his gaze to where his shaft pierced Elijah's body and slowed his movements.

"Beautiful," Carter growled.

Elijah followed his gaze and moaned, his hole clenching reflexively around Carter's swollen organ.

They both panted as Carter drew his cock out slowly, the surface glistening wetly with his precum, the rim of Elijah's hole clinging lovingly to his flesh.

"Every inch of you is goddamn beautiful."

Carter slammed back in with enough force to raise Elijah up against the wall.

White light exploded in front of Elijah's eyes, his mouth opening on a cry of ecstasy. Then Carter's mouth was on his, muffling their animal sounds while he withdrew and thrust back in again and again, his movements hard and deep.

Carter's lips swallowed Elijah's hoarse cries as the latter finally climaxed, dick shooting cum all the way up their chests. The strong convulsions ripping through Elijah's ass finally tipped Carter over the edge and he came with fury, his hips pumping wildly.

Elijah whimpered when he felt Carter's cock pulse and throb repeatedly deep inside him, drenching his passage with a pool of cum.

Carter's hips finally slowed. Violent shudders shook him as he lifted his mouth from Elijah's and dropped his forehead against his.

They both looked down when Carter slowly pulled out, his dick now liberally coated with his own cum.

"Fuck, that's sexy," Carter mumbled. "I could get used to this."

Elijah moaned and squeezed his hole as Carter slowly lowered him to the floor, still stunned by the whole experience. He leaned against Carter, his entire body quaking with the aftermath of their lovemaking.

"I could get used to this too," Elijah panted against Carter's shoulder. Heat flooded his face when he felt the remains of Carter's cum trickle down the inside of his thighs. "Sex with you is amazing but that was something—*oh!*"

Carter's fingers had found his pleasantly used pucker and was carefully cleaning him out.

Elijah clutched at his wrist. "You—you don't have to—!"

"Yes, I do." Carter kissed him tenderly, his expression determined. "You're my partner. Let me take care of you."

Elijah dropped his head against the shoulder of the man he loved and let him do just that, his heart full to bursting.

CHAPTER THIRTY

Carter drummed his fingers on his knee.

"Nervous?" Barbara murmured where she sat opposite him.

"A little bit," Carter admitted.

The door opened. One of Carter's lawyers stepped in.

"They're ready for you."

Carter dipped his chin, took a deep breath, and rose to his feet. He adjusted his cuffs and tie before following his agent and his lawyers out of the room.

They were in one of the most famous hotels in Beverly Hills, about to deliver what Carter felt confident would be the conference of a lifetime.

A week had passed since the world found out he was bisexual. The outpouring of support that had followed the breakout story had stunned Carter. Not only were his fans strong advocates of his rights to do as he wanted in his private life, they had also been angry when they'd found out he'd been dropped from his latest movie and vowed to shun the studio's future projects.

Carter was also humbled by the personal messages of encouragement he'd received from veterans of the industry and new actors alike, everyone congratulating him on his relationship and expressing their outrage at what the studio had done.

One of the studio executives had contacted Barbara the day before and asked if he could speak to Carter. She had accompanied him to the late night meeting and had been as staggered as the man they'd gone to see when Carter produced some information he had so far kept to himself.

"Why didn't you tell me about this earlier? Or your lawyers even?!"

Carter gazed at his agent apologetically, conscious of the studio executive's pale face on the other side of the desk.

"Because it's a dirty trick and one that I wouldn't wish was pulled on me. I would only have submitted it as evidence had we decided to go to court."

The executive's face grew even paler. Carter turned to him.

"I appreciate this meeting, Ben. I realize the studio wished to protect itself from the fallout of this story."

The man nodded. "I'm glad we managed to resolve it. And I'm truly sorry. About what happened last week and about this latest development. I'll be sure to let the studio directors know what transpired here tonight."

"I'm giving a press conference tomorrow," Carter said.

The man startled. His expression grew resigned. "Will

you be showing them what you've just showed to me and Barbara?"

Carter hesitated. "I will. She'll do this to other people. Probably has already. Someone needs to make a stand."

"You know this will destroy her reputation?"

Carter gazed steadily at the studio executive. "She had no qualms about crushing mine."

The man sighed. "Fair enough."

"Ready?" Barbara said presently.

They'd stopped in front of a door. A low roar came from the other side.

Carter nodded at the agent. She opened the door.

Cameras flashed. A hundred voices clamored at Carter.

He kept his expression neutral and walked up to the stage that had been set up at the head of the conference hall, Barbara and his lawyers at his side. They headed behind the long table bearing microphones and settled in their seats.

The uproar slowly abated.

One of his lawyers spoke. "Mr. Wilson will not be taking any questions from the floor. He called this conference to make a statement about what happened last week. We would appreciate your cooperation in letting him speak uninterrupted."

Another clamor broke out as the reporters protested wildly.

Carter arched an eyebrow, tilted his mouth in the arrogant half-smile Hollywood knew him for, and leaned toward one of the mikes.

"You guys. I appreciate that you've all come here

today for some juicy gossip. But you're not getting any until you've piped the hell down."

Laughter broke out in the audience.

"Way to handle them like a pro," Barbara murmured next to him.

The atmosphere got visibly less fraught and the din subsided.

"Thank you." Carter looked out over the room. Some of the faces he was familiar with, having granted them interviews over the years. There were also a number of international gossip columnists that he knew by reputation only.

Carter studied the crowd for a moment, conscious of the dozens of cameras and voice recorders trained on him. In the past, he had imagined all sorts of scenarios if and when the story of his bisexuality broke out. In all of them, he would be an utter mess at this point.

Yet, he had never felt calmer. Because inside the inner pocket of his suit, pressed against his very heart, was a jewelry box containing the ring he intended to give Elijah tonight.

Carter composed his thoughts and started to talk.

CHAPTER THIRTY-ONE

Elijah drew a shallow breath and clenched his fingers together as he watched the man speaking on TV. He was sitting in the bakery's break room, watching the live conference. Sam and Nico sat on either side of him, their gazes riveted to the screen.

"He said it," Sam breathed.

"Don't know why it took so long," Nico grumbled.

Elijah cut his eyes to the French chef.

Nico sighed. "All right, I'll shut up."

"If you were expecting me to deny that fact, then I'm sorry to tell you that you were wrong," Carter continued on screen, his voice steady. "As to why I kept this a secret for so long, I think last week's shitstorm is more than enough proof that I had good reason to."

Chuckles broke out from among the crowd of reporters.

Carter let out an exasperated sigh and smiled. "I get

that you guys are doing your jobs, but you can be a real pain in the ass, you know that? And yes, I am aware that I just said ass in the context of being gay."

This got a roar of laughter.

"He really knows how to work the room, doesn't he?" Nico muttered. "Charismatic asshole."

Elijah stared unblinkingly at the screen, his pulse racing. All he could see was the man he loved, being himself.

"Being bisexual is not something I'm ashamed of, contrary to the stories that have been circulating in the media this past week. My friends and my family are fully aware of my sexual preferences and have been for the last ten years. My decision to not come out of the closet to the rest of the world had everything to do with the career I had chosen to dedicate my life to."

Carter took a deep breath.

"There is no denying that there is still a lot of prejudice against people like me in this industry. But I am also conscious that there are a *lot* of people like me in this business. And I am eternally grateful to everyone who'd reached out to me in the last few days to express their support. I hope the movement I'm joining will continue to bring change to our workplace practices and reshape preconceived ideas. On that note, I have an announcement to make. I will be resuming work on the project that I was dropped from last week shortly."

Shocked murmurs broke out across the conference room.

Elijah bit his lip. Sam and Nico turned to him, surprise pasted across their faces.

"Did you know?" Sam asked.

Elijah nodded. "He told me when he came home last night."

Carter waited until the noise died down before speaking again. "I also have a message." He turned to face the closest camera to him. "Mira, I didn't want to have to do this, but you left me with little choice when you hired that reporter to spy on me. This is not just for me, but for every actor who will cross your path and who you will ruin with your selfishness." He took his cell out, brought something up, and laid the device on table. He tilted the microphone slightly and tapped the cellphone's screen.

A recording started to play.

Elijah sucked in air as he listened to the voice echoing from the phone and across the TV speakers. Even though he'd never met Mira, he knew it was her. And he knew exactly what day Carter had taped that clip.

The conference room went deathly quiet.

"Holy shit!" Sam blurted halfway through the recording.

Nico scowled. "Did she just blackmail him into sleeping with her? What a bitch."

Anger coiled through Elijah. Although Carter had told him what had happened that day, the reality of it was still chilling.

And he never said he'd recorded her.

Another uproar broke out after Carter stopped the clip. He waited until it abated before talking again.

"I had every intention of suing Mira Peters for defamation. But I realized it would only lead to more grief and would keep me away from the people I love." Carter paused and stared at the camera he'd been looking into earlier, a soft smile on his lips. "From the little girl I adore. From the friends I cherish. And from the man I love and intend to marry."

Elijah knew that Carter was talking to him in that moment.

There was a breathless pause. The conference room exploded with the flash of dozens of cameras and a storm of excited shouts.

Carter ignored the uproar and kept staring into the camera, his smile widening.

"*He proposed?!*" Sam squealed.

"That bastard!" Nico growled.

Armando and Daisy burst into the break room a moment later, the cell phones in their hands streaming the now very loud live conference.

"You're gonna marry Carter Wilson?!" the quarterback gasped.

Elijah sighed. "Aren't you two supposed to be manning the shop?"

"Answer the question!" Sam demanded.

Elijah grimaced as he became the focus of a battery of stares. He rubbed the back of his neck awkwardly.

"Yes, I'm going to marry Carter."

Carter turned up when the bakery was closing for the day.

Elijah had just finished wiping down the surfaces when a key sounded in the back door. He turned just as Carter stepped inside the kitchen.

Carter closed and locked the door before strolling toward him.

"Hey. Did Maisie settle in okay at Izzy's?"

"Yeah. She called a while back. Maisie had dinner and went to sleep." Elijah smiled and put down the towel. "That was quite something."

Carter grinned, leaned against the counter next to Elijah, and crossed his ankles. He was still wearing his suit from the conference.

Elijah couldn't help admire how the material hugged his athletic body. His ears warmed when he recalled exactly how that body had felt against him, above him, under him, and inside him over the last week of their endless lovemaking.

Rock hard. Sinful. And sexy as hell.

"I don't know what you're thinking about right now, but that look on your face really makes me want to kiss you," Carter blurted.

Elijah stepped in front of Carter, braced his hands on either side of his body, and tilted his head to nibble teasingly at his jawline.

"What's stopping you, stud?"

Carter arched a haughty eyebrow. "Stud?"

Elijah nodded. "Uh-huh. Your stamina is pretty scary." He nipped at Carter's lower lip and smiled when he saw desire pool in the heated hazel eyes opposite him. "I have a feeling I should start working out too."

Carter fake pouted. "But I like you just the way you

are." He sneaked his arms around Elijah and pulled him into his embrace. "Gotcha!"

Elijah chuckled. "What are you going to do to me now that you have me?"

Carter's expression grew solemn. "I will cherish every moment I have with you. And I will hold you, from this day forward, for better, for worse. For richer, for poorer. In sickness and in health. Until—"

"Death do us part," Elijah whispered against Carter's lips, his eyes welling with tears, his chest full to bursting.

They kissed, slowly, deeply, reverently, as if they stood inside a church, making their vows in front of God.

Their breathing was ragged when they lifted their mouths off one another.

Carter slipped a hand inside his suit and took out a small satin box.

Elijah's eyes widened when he opened it, exposing a pair of beautiful titanium rings with a discrete line of sparkling, black onyx stones.

Carter took one of the bands and slipped it on Elijah's left ring finger.

It fit perfectly.

"Will you do mine?" Carter said in a low voice, his eyes blazing with love.

Elijah nodded shakily. He took the second ring and put it on Carter's finger.

They linked their hands and gazed at the matching rings.

"I love them," Elijah mumbled.

Carter kissed the tip of his nose. "I'm glad you do."

Elijah leaned into Carter, so happy he wanted to pinch himself. His grandmother had been right. He'd found everything he ever wanted, right here in Twilight Falls.

Carter shifted slightly.

Elijah chuckled. "If you're attempting to hide that raging erection, you're doing a very poor job of it."

Carter groaned. "I can't help it. You're in my arms and I can smell your scent. It's enough to drive a sane man out of his mind."

Elijah stepped back and reached for the top of his chef uniform. "In case you hadn't noticed, I'm hard too." He raised an eyebrow as he slowly popped the buttons open, his heart pounding at the open love and lust painted across Carter's face. "I believe you once fantasized about making love to me in this uniform, didn't you?"

Carter cursed and reached for Elijah, his movements desperate.

Then the actor had his very, *very* wicked way with the chef.

THE END

Can a business rival bring one of Twilight Falls' most notorious bad boys to his knees?
notorious bad boys to his knees?
Get Hunter (Twilight Falls 3)

Have you read the Nights series yet? Get One Night (Nights #1) and find out if Gabe Anderson accepts Cam Sorvino's promise of one night of mindless pleasure to help him overcome his phobia of intimacy!
Get One Night (Nights 1)
Turn the page to read an extract now!

What the hell am I doing here?

Gabe Anderson scanned the crowded club in the mirror opposite the bar before looking down into his scotch with a self-deprecating smile. This had seemed like such a great idea an hour ago, when he'd been staring at an empty weekend in an even emptier apartment.

Saron was located in a side alley, a short walk from Shinjuku's main club strip. Despite its somewhat shady location, the place oozed style.

Gabe had hesitated when he'd seen the suited doorman guarding the entrance and wondered if access was by invitation only. He only knew of *Saron* from overhearing his clients mention it a few nights ago. From what he'd made of their excited conversation, it was *the* place to hang out in Shinjuku if you were of a particular sexual inclination.

The doorman had checked Gabe over for all of three seconds before wordlessly unclipping the rope from the stanchions framing the steel doors. He had obviously passed some kind of test, though what it was he didn't know.

Beyond a foyer with a cloakroom manned by a male attendant who looked like he'd walked straight out of a *GQ* shoot were a set of shallow steps leading to a wide, sunken floor.

Despite the butterflies churning his stomach, Gabe had stopped and stared appreciatively at the decor. As a consultant for one of Chicago's biggest design firms, he could tell how much money had gone into giving *Saron* its unique look. The club was drowned in deep reds, dark purples, and rich earth tones. Scattered across the oak floor were Brazilian cherry wood tables and armchairs boasting plush velvet upholstery and satin cushions. Discrete booths dotted the walls and afforded privacy to those who needed it, although the muted lighting provided enough of that as it was. A polished mahogany counter with wine-red leather and walnut stools ran the length of the bar on the right.

At the far end of the room, a woman in a black cocktail dress stood on a raised podium. She was crooning a song in a sultry, deep voice, her eyes closed and her glossy ruby lips glistening in the mellow spotlight. Behind her, cymbals vibrated gently, a piano tinkled, and a saxophone hummed, the sounds somehow rising above the voices of the men packing the place.

It was as he'd made his way to the bar that Gabe had realized why the doorman had let him in. From the looks of the club's patrons, *Saron* catered exclusively to an upscale clientele. He was willing to bet a week's wages none of the suits in the place cost less than five hundred dollars.

"Ah, fresh meat."

Gabe froze in the act of sitting on a barstool, his gaze swinging up to meet a pair of amused green eyes on the other side of the mahogany counter.

"Excuse me?" he said stiffly.

The bartender, a striking blond in a slate, silk tuxedo vest and crisp white shirt, flashed him a grin.

"I've not seen you around these parts before. What will it be?"

Gabe swallowed, wondering whether the man had seen straight through him and grasped the reason he had come to *Saron*.

"What will what be?" he mumbled, unable to mask the apprehension in his voice.

The bartender pursed his lips and observed him with a shrewd expression before leaning across the counter.

"Relax," he murmured in Gabe's left ear. "I can tell it's your first time in a place like this. If you keep up that deer-in-the-headlights look you've got painted across that pretty face of yours, you're gonna be a target for every sleaze ball in this club. And, trust me, they might be wearing thousand-dollar ensembles, but some of these assholes are nothing but dirty pigs in suits."

An involuntary bark of laughter left Gabe's lips at the mental image the bartender's words had conjured. The sound carried along the counter, drawing stares.

The knot of tension that had been sitting between Gabe's shoulder blades ever since he ventured into Shinjuku eased as he smiled at the bartender.

"I've never been called pretty before."

The guy winked.

"Trust me, you're the hottest thing on legs in this place right now. Besides me, of course."

Gabe chuckled and ordered a scotch, his confidence boosted by the compliment.

Two months had passed since he'd relocated to Tokyo from Chicago. When his bosses had sprung the offer on Gabe in early spring, the chance of a fresh start in a place void of the dark memories that had plagued him for eight years was too much of an attractive proposition for him to reject. He'd left Chicago with two suitcases and five crates full of books and artwork, the only things he had to show after a decade in the city.

Though he had been prepared for the culture shock, life in Tokyo had still come as a surprise, albeit an invigorating one. He had always had an interest in the country and its intoxicating mix of traditional and contemporary customs ever since he made his first business trip to the Japanese branch of the firm four years ago.

Luckily, his new position suited him to a T. He had thrown himself into his first assignment with his usual drive and passion, leading the team under him to make good on a project, one which his predecessor had only made a half-assed attempt to complete. He had delivered on time, on budget, and on schedule, despite the nearly impossible deadline. The crazy hours and weekends he had put in had not gone unnoticed, and the praise lavished on his team at the grand opening of their client's luxury hotel earlier that week was all the acknowledgment Gabe needed to realize he had made the right choice in moving to this city. The fact that the money he was making could easily afford him a two-bedroom condo in the exclusive neighborhood of Meguro didn't hurt, either.

Yet, despite having relocated thousands of miles to the other side of the world, his mind would not let go of the bite of his past. Which was why, when faced with the prospect of his first free weekend and the boxes he had yet to unpack, he had looked up *Saron's* location on the spur of the moment and decided to take a gamble.

He had promised himself this move would not be just a fresh start for his mind, but for his body, too. That he would start taking risks in his personal life again. That he would not let the bastard who had made it impossible for him to ever have a satisfying physical relationship win.

Fifteen minutes into his first drink and Gabe wondered whether he had made a bad choice. So far, Ethan, the bartender, had helped him field a burly, yakuza-looking type with tattoos up the side of his neck, three old men with sweaty palms and bald patches, and a couple of young guys who looked barely past the legal age of drinking.

With his lean build, dark hair, and blue eyes, Gabe knew he was an attractive prospect. Add in that he was a foreigner and he was coming to the conclusion that he had become a beeline for all the men in the bar who wanted to make a conquest out of the white guy – a white notch in the proverbial bedpost. They all wanted to fuck him or be fucked by him.

A cynical half-smile twisted his lips at that thought. If only they knew.

He raised a hand to the back of his neck and rubbed the warm spot that had been bothering him for a while. Something made him look up from his drink then – call it instinct or that subconscious voice that warns of imminent danger. Movement in the mirror opposite the bar caught his gaze. Or, more precisely, a lack of it.

Stormy gray eyes pierced him from the other end of the club. They locked on him, a beam of light in the gloom. Transfixing him. Immobilizing him.

Gabe's breath caught in his throat, every muscle in his body tightening in fight-or-flight mode.

The man sat apart from the crowd, alone at a table that could have accommodated three, a tumbler full of dark liquid clasped casually in his left hand. His red silk tie was crooked, as if he had slipped a finger through the knot to loosen it. The top two buttons on his white shirt were open, revealing tan skin covering toned muscles and a hint of curls.

Gabe couldn't tell whether his hair was dark brown or dirty blond. It was hard to say in the dim light. What wasn't hard to see were the subtle and not-so-subtle stares the other men in the bar were giving the stranger.

With his stubbled face, smoldering looks, and what appeared to be an incredibly ripped body beneath a custom-tailored charcoal suit, the man looked like a king sitting on a throne, commanding a roomful of servants. Servants who appeared more than willing to either get fucked by him or fuck him if he so much as lifted his little finger.

And a man like that would not have to ask twice.

Envy and irritation flashed through Gabe at that thought, shattering the spell he found himself under. He broke eye contact, shocked by the feelings suddenly flooding him, and glared at his half-empty glass. It seemed to mock him, as if it were a reflection of his own life. A half-empty, broken shell. Incapable of touching someone or to be touched.

Gabe lifted the glass and downed the rest of the drink with an angry flick of his wrist. Fire singed his throat. He welcomed the burning sensation, hoping it would calm the pounding in his chest and the tightness in his belly and groin that told him his body had reacted to the stranger.

A full glass of scotch appeared next to his empty tumbler.

Gabe looked up at Ethan, puzzled.

A remorseful grimace flashed across the bartender's face. "Looks like we're no longer the two hottest bastards in this joint. Here, compliments of the King."

Gabe stared at the drink before slowly looking over his shoulder, his pulse picking up speed.

Gray Eyes raised his glass in a toast. A teasing smile played on his sculptured lips before he knocked back his drink.

You're kidding me.

Gabe tried to block out the heated tingle running across his skin at the stranger's cocky smirk and the way his powerful throat muscles worked when he swallowed. He turned to Ethan.

"That's his *actual* name?"

Ethan grunted. "Well, no. But the asshole sure acts like one."

There was movement in the mirror opposite Gabe.

Read One Night today

AFTERWORD

To all my friends who helped make this possible. You know who you are.

To you, my readers. Thank you for reading Carter and Elijah's story. I hope you loved the second book in the Twilight Falls series. I would be grateful if you could leave a review on Goodreads or on the store where you purchased this book. Reviews help readers like you find my books and I truly appreciate your honest opinions about my stories.

Make sure to sign up to my store newsletter for special deals on my books and new release alerts. Or you can sign up to my author newsletter instead to get upcoming release notifications, sneak peeks, and giveaways.